THE LAST GUN

Jack Crawford, badly wounded in the final action of the Civil War, returns home to discover that his parents have been massacred, and the family ranch has fallen into the hands of empire-building newcomer Vic Bannon. When Crawford becomes town sheriff, he finds himself in opposition to the ruthless Bannon, with his own brother Clay helping to force the homesteaders and farmers out of the valley. As the threat of range war looms, Crawford must defend the home he now barely recognizes, before it disappears forever.

F 202 04701 X 1234

PETER WILSON

◆

THE
LAST GUN

Complete and Unabridged

LINFORD
Leicester

First published in Great Britain in 2015 by
Robert Hale Limited
London

First Linford Edition
published 2018
by arrangement with
Robert Hale
an imprint of The Crowood Press
Wiltshire

A catalogue record for this book is available
from the British Library.

ISBN 978–1–4448–3761–2

Published by
F. A. Thorpe (Publishing)
Anstey, Leicestershire

Set by Words & Graphics Ltd.
Anstey, Leicestershire
Printed and bound in Great Britain by
T. J. International Ltd., Padstow, Cornwall

This book is printed on acid-free paper

The Last Gun

Cannon smoke darkened the skies and the screams of young men dying in battle added to the horrors of the afternoon. The fresh-faced young lieutenant, just three days short of his twenty-fourth birthday, scrambled towards a group of men crouched in a hollow to his left.

The war was nearing its lingering end; defeat was written all over the muddied faces and the blood-stained grey uniforms of the men facing despair.

'Mack's gone, sir,' the first man said, his voice a gasping rattle.

The young officer said nothing. Instead he crawled up the grassy slope to survey the battlefield. He knew that the town of Mobile would already have been taken by the Federal troops, leaving Fort Blakely as the final stronghold of the Confederacy. And he knew that could not hold for many hours longer. They were heavily out-numbered and the man they called Mack was just the latest on a growing list of casualties.

He rolled over on to his back and stared up at the smoke-filled sky.

'What in the name of all that's holy are we doing here?' He had asked the same question many times over the last six days but was no closer to an answer.

What had started as a cause he felt worthy was turning into a massacre of young men and innocent civilians. Nearby, a trooper yelled an obscenity as he suddenly rushed from the safety of his cover, screaming and firing blindly into the afternoon. The young lieuten-ant could only watch as the man was cut down in mid-stride.

'Poor bastard,' a soldier muttered.

'He's a lucky one,' another man said. 'He's out of it.'

A further burst of cannon fire drowned the other man's response. It was then that the first bullet ripped

2

through the young officer's left shoulder. A second bullet caught him in the thigh. The third should have ended his life but instead it sent him spinning unconscious against an embankment.

An hour later, General Robert E. Lee signed the declaration. The war was over.

1

The voices were distant but clear.

'What do you think, Doc? Will he come through?'

The medical man turned to look at the stricken figure strapped to the makeshift bed. He felt for the young man.

'Well, I have done all I can, Major, but he's one of the lucky ones. If he pulls through at least he will come out of this senseless war with all his limbs. But, as for his survival? The rest is up to the Good Lord.'

The man in the grey uniform sighed.

'The Good Lord hasn't been looking too kindly on us much these past few months, Doc. I reckon that maybe he owes us this one. It's as well that the poor guy can't hear us and don't know what we just heard. That General Lee has signed the surrender.'

He looked around at the rows of wounded men and sighed again.

'What was it all for? Four years of blood-spilling; hundreds of thousands killed or wounded and that kid there closer to death than life. Do you know, Doc, I really believed that we were in the right, that Abe Lincoln had taken a step too far but now, well, I don't know. Was it really worth it?'

The major and the doctor left the room and the young man on the bed remained still. He had heard. The war was over. The South — *his* people, *his* family — had lost. Four years of conflict costing so many lives and homes, had come to an end at the stroke of a pen.

His pain-wracked body could take no more. He closed his eyes in an attempt to stem the flow of tears.

'Will he come through?' the major had asked. Was it really up to the Lord as the doctor had suggested? Had those bullets that had ripped through his body in another pointless skirmish done so much damage?

He was just three days short of his twenty-fourth birthday when it had happened. Three bullets: one in the leg, one in the shoulder and, as he turned to dive for cover, one in the back.

But he had survived, if lying here waiting for death was survival. The blackness of unconsciousness was a blessing.

*   *   *

The strength of the storm was increasing by the minute and the four passengers in the stage exchanged nervous glances.

They were a divergent quartet of travellers. No names and few words had been exchanged since the start of the journey now in its sixteenth hour. By noon tomorrow the stage would pull into Creek Forks and the four would go their separate ways, but for now, the strengthening winds and driving rain would force them to make an unscheduled stop at the next trading post.

The oldest of the four, a ruddy-faced man dressed in a brown checked suit, had slept for the past hour and only stirred when the stage hit a loose rock on the road.

Opposite him, the young woman's face betrayed a sense of fear as the storm unleashed another lightning flash, quickly followed by a clap of thunder and biting rain, which splashed through the curtain of the coach window.

Beside her, the black-cloaked clergyman continued to read his Bible, occasionally muttering a private prayer. He was a pale, thin-faced man — hooked nose, lank hair, dark drooping moustache and receding stubble-covered chin — possibly even a figure of fun for the young kids who gathered outside his places of worship. The reverend was not a happy man.

The fourth member of the travelling group was a young, fair-haired man who stared vacantly ahead as if deep in thought.

Indeed, thoughts of what lay ahead were what had occupied Jack Crawford for two painful years — since that black day when he stopped three Union bullets.

'Best hold on tight, young lady, we're in for a rough ride.'

The suited figure's voice broke into Jack's daydreaming. When the young woman did not answer, the man leaned forward and touched her arm.

'Don't you worry, miss. We'll soon be at Jackson's Point and — '

Another flash of lightning and a thunder crack sent a shudder through the young passenger and the clergyman was sent spinning from his seat.

'God preserve us and spare us from your wrath!' he chanted.

The man in the brown suit chuckled.

'That's right, Reverend, you tell your boss we're in a hole down here.' He turned his attention back to the woman. 'We're gonna be fine, miss, the reverend's getting help.'

The stagecoach rocked and swayed as the driver fought to keep his team of four under control. It was a losing battle. For almost an hour the stage was buffeted by the fierce winds and rain and the passengers were swung violently in their seats. Up front the driver and his shotgun partner struggled to handle their frightened horses.

Throughout the ride, the young man in the corner never spoke. Instead, he suffered in silence as the pain from his leg wound increased to an almost unbearable pitch — a reminder of the closing hours of a lost war.

★　★　★

Joe Jackson had been running his trading post for almost twenty years and he was well accustomed to the regular visits from stage passengers caught in a storm or too weary to continue their journey, so he was fully prepared when the Southlander rattled into the holding paddock outside his three-roomed building shortly after nightfall.

Shouting above the roar of the storm, he waved to his son Charlie to get the horses into the barn.

'And make sure to wipe them down good, son,' he yelled. 'They'll all be here for the night.'

Inside the building that had survived many storms like tonight's, Sarah Jackson was already setting the table, stoking the fire and checking that there was enough food for the six unexpected visitors who were already staggering in out of the rain.

She knew driver Matt Dawson and his shotgun rider Dave Reagan well enough to know that they would settle for what was left after she had fed the paying customers. The rest were strangers: the thin, sharp-featured reverend clutching his Bible as though Armageddon was only hours away; the pretty young woman who looked pale with fear; the round-faced man in the brown suit who blustered his way towards the fire; and the fourth member of the party, a fair-haired young man with a slight limp, who occasionally needed a cane to give him support — he looked vaguely familiar but Sarah could not think where she might have seen him before.

'Supper will be ready in ten minutes, folks, meantime, make yourselves comfortable.'

Nobody answered but the man in the suit hogged the seat closest to the fire.

Charlie came in from the barn and proudly announced that he had settled the horses down for the night and added that the storm was showing no signs of easing.

'We'll be fine here for the night,' Dawson said, 'and we will make an early start and should be pulling into Creek Forks around about noon tomorrow.'

'That's a whole day late,' the clergyman grumbled, still clutching The Good Book.

'I'm sure your flock will wait for you, Padre,' the man in the suit scoffed. 'Besides, it's your boss's fault we're stuck out here in the middle of nowhere.'

The young girl and the man with the limp settled at the table and waited for the food to arrive. There was little conversation between the travelers, who had been confined to the inside of a stage for six hours without a break since the previous staging post.

Joe Jackson did his best to make them feel at home. Like his wife, he too had the feeling that he knew the limping man from somewhere. It was only when he was helping to clear away the empty dinner plates that the memory came back. He slid into an empty chair beside the young man. He had a look of minor triumph on his face.

'Ain't you Billy Crawford's young 'un? Rancher out Creek Forks way?'

For the first time, Jack Crawford raised a smile.

'That's me, Mr Jackson.'

They shook hands.

'Lord, it must be ten years since I saw you.'

'More like fourteen, Mr Jackson. I was only twelve when you came into town. Your son Charlie there wasn't even born.'

'Fourteen years! Now look at you.'

He spotted the cane standing by Jack's chair.

'The war?' he asked, gesturing towards the cane.

Jack nodded. 'Mobile, Alabama.'

Joe shook his head. 'Damn bad luck, son. The war was all over by then and you poor guys didn't even know it. Where have you been these last two years?'

Jack sipped his coffee.

'The doctors needed that much time to put me back together so I've been in hospital most of it, learning to walk again.'

'So, you're heading home?'

'Sure am, and I can't wait to see the

old place again. It's been almost five years.'

The trading post owner lowered his eyes and with that his voice.

'You'll see a lot of changes, Jack, especially since . . . well, since your folks . . . 'His voice tailed away as though he could not bring himself to say what was on his mind. Instead he muttered: 'A terrible day. Terrible.'

Jack had had no contact with his family since early in the second year of the war. His decision to join the Confederate forces had hit Billy and Martha badly and their sons had had a bitter fight over the decision.

'You're needed here — not getting yourself killed in some crazy war,' his mother had argued. 'Clay and your father can't do all that's needed around the ranch. We need you.'

But the plea had been in vain and Jack's departure had been a bitter occasion. His brother Clay had branded him a deserter even before he joined the army.

'Running out on your folks, Jack, that's desertion.'

Now he was heading home, the bad times would be forgotten and the Crawfords would be a family again.

'What is it, Joe? What are you trying to tell me?'

The trading post boss did not answer at once.

'I — I thought you would know, Jack. It's been four years. I thought you would know.'

'What is it, Joe? What should I know?'

'Four years ago your place was attacked. There was nothing anybody could do. Your mom and dad. They're dead, Jack. They were killed by a group of rebel deserters. Some of Quantrill's gang.'

2

All the letters that Jack Crawford had written from his hospital bed had gone unanswered. His sorrow at the way he had left the family ranch; his efforts to heal the rift with his elder brother; the report of his wounds and his memories of a futile war — all written for nothing.

Now, as he sat silently in the stage, staring out at the ragged landscape, he reflected on what Joe Jackson had told him the previous night.

His parents, burned out of their home by a group of deserters, killers in grey uniforms, men from his own side. For two years he had fought alongside such men in the name of the Confederate States. Friends had died, horribly, violently for the cause of the South. Men with families, brothers, sisters, some even with children of their own.

Jack Crawford had seen so many of them die.

Until that point, the war had ended for him on that final day at Fort Berkeley, outside of Mobile Alabama. But for Jack Crawford the war still had one more cruel twist: the death of his peace-loving parents.

His brother had been away on ranch errands — the sort of duty that Jack would have been expected to do — when the raiders struck but, according to Joe Jackson, the deaths had hit Clay hard and he was a changed man.

Joe would say nothing more but Jack's feeling was that the trading post boss recognized that the changes in Clay had not been for the better.

'It's not for me to judge your brother, Jack, but you will know for yourself soon enough.'

The storm had long gone and it was a fine sunny morning when the stage rolled along the last few miles of its journey north to the town of Creek Forks.

'The war did cruel things to us all, Mr Crawford. My brother was killed at Bull Run. I'm very sorry for your loss.'

It was the young woman's voice that broke into Jack's thoughts. He turned to face her. She was exceptionally pretty: a pale face of high cheekbones, a generous mouth that would have offered the perfect smile and big blue eyes. He had hardly even noticed her the previous night.

'I'm sorry, Miss . . . ?'

'Jenny. Jenny Lang.'

She gave him a smile and it was what he had expected. Perfect.

'My brother was in the army. Not the same as you, of course. He was in the Federal Army.'

'We're all in the United States now, Miss Lang,' Jack said quietly although he was still unsure whether he believed it.

'You don't sound too happy about that, young man,' the clergyman broke in. 'I'm Reverend Abel Child. We all have to live together. The war has been over for two years.'

Jack gave him a fixed stare. 'Reverend, I have just heard that both my parents are dead and I don't need any preacher to tell me what to think.'

Undaunted, Abel Child pressed on. 'I understand. War wounds not only the body. It gets through to the soul and mind. There are times when we must be brave; to search in our hearts to forgive the people who — '

'Leave the kid alone, Padre. Let him hurt in his own way,' the man in the brown checked suit snapped.

The four fell silent again and Jack Crawford returned to staring out at the passing landscape. He guessed they would be arriving at Creek Forks in less than an hour. Then he would have the chance to see for himself the many changes that Joe Jackson had talked about at the dinner table the previous night.

★   ★   ★

Sheriff Luke Franklin was drunk. The truth was he had not been fully sober for days. Ever since a young kid was shot and he had been advised — no, ordered — to turn his suspect loose. Except that he was not just a suspect. Everybody in town knew that Blake Bannon had done the killing but Bannon was the son of an important man around the territory.

Little Lester Thomas was a known petty thief and rowdy; there was no chance of a case being brought. He stole only enough to help keep his sickly grandmother alive and nobody saw the actual killing. Nobody ever saw anything in Creek Forks that would make life more difficult if they chose to speak out.

Luke Franklin had turned into such a man. It was true, the money was good — three times what he could earn as a lawman in any other town — but it had cost him his wife and his son hated his guts.

So he drank, and with the drinking

came a mixture of self-pity and self-loathing. He poured himself another whiskey and watched the incoming stage roll slowly past his office window on the way to the depot at the end of Main Street.

There was a time, before the war, when he would have been up off his seat and down the street to greet new arrivals and collect his mail.

But not today — things had changed.

There were only two people at the depot to greet the long-delayed stage — a middle-aged couple who took it in turns to wrap their arms around Jenny Lang.

The Reverend Abel Child stepped down, stretched his thin frame, sniffed the air, grabbed without thanks his carpet bag from the stage driver and headed back along the street the way they had come. They had passed a small, neglected church on their way into town. But that was not the destination for the grim-faced man in black. He had other business to attend to before looking over the centre of worship. Saving the souls of the sinners of Creek Forks would have to wait for another day.

The man in the brown suit strode purposefully across the street and marched up the steps into what Jack Crawford remembered as the Flag Hotel. The nameplate had disappeared from above the door and had been replaced by a garish-coloured sign that announced: Aces High Casino Bar. A quick glance around confirmed for Jack that the new name for the town's hotel was not the only change.

The building next to the Flag Hotel — a small, hardware and grain store — was boarded up, as was the family-run café down the street. Apart from a couple of brightly painted buildings, Creek Forks had all the appearance of a decaying, run-down town.

Jack took his baggage from the stage and headed down the street to the one place he hoped would still be unchanged and where he would get a warm welcome.

Whatever other changes had taken place since he left to join the army, Jack was confident that Ma Bailey's guest house would still be in business.

Alice Bailey was Jack's aunt — his father's sister — and had been running Creek Forks' only clean, well-kept accommodation ever since her husband was killed in the Mexican Wars of 1848. Jack had been only six years old at the time; his brother was already old enough to help out around the ranch so Jack had spent a lot of his time with Aunt Alice while his father built up the Circle-C and his mother helped out around the general store.

On the walk along Main Street Jack came across several faces he recognized but none acknowledged his casual greeting. Perhaps it was the cane, the slight limp, or the clothes, maybe the way he had filled out since he last strolled among the residents of his home town.

Whatever the reason, Jack Crawford was just another anonymous stranger among many others that bright, sunny fall afternoon.

Ma Bailey's guest house was indeed still in business but she was not at home. Instead, Jack's knock on the door was answered by a young boy, maybe thirteen or fourteen years old.

'Mrs Bailey's not here, mister,' the boy said sullenly. No hint of a greeting smile but Jack knew the lad.

'It's Tommy, isn't it? Tommy Carter.'

The boy looked hard in the face of the visitor.

'Do I know you, mister?'

'Probably not. You were only six or seven years old the last time I saw you.'

'I'm thirteen now. But I still don't know you.' He looked at Jack's stick. 'You hurt your leg?'

'Just a bit, but it's getting better every day.'

'Anyways, like I said, Mrs Bailey ain't here right now. You'll have to come back later.'

Jack smiled. 'Fine, Tommy, but will you tell her I called and I'll be back?'

'I'll tell her. But what name should I say?'

'Tell her Jack called. Jack Crawford.'

The boy stared long and hard into Jack's face. It was almost as if the sound of the name had hit him full in the stomach.

'Crawford? Right, mister, I'll let her know,' he said at last. 'But I reckon you should not come back later. Ma won't want to know.'

He quickly backed into the house, slamming the door and leaving a bewildered Jack on the porch steps.

⋆　⋆　⋆

In the eyes of most townsfolk of Creek Forks, Alice Bailey was not a woman to be crossed. Stubborn and strong-willed, Alice had come through many hardships during her fifty-seven years and had made much of her life since her husband's death at the hands of the

Mexicans at the Alamo fighting alongside Jim Bowie and Davy Crockett.

Her neatly kept boarding house offered accommodation as comfortable as the more expensive Flag Hotel and her general store had supplied most of the needs of the local people for years, all the products coming from her smallholding of chickens, dairy cows and pigs outside of town.

Alice was a wiry, muscular woman with a booming voice and a temper to match any man's. She was more loved and admired than liked and her accuracy with a shotgun or six-shooter was famous the length and breadth of the county. But all that had changed when, in the third year of the war, her brother and his wife were burned out of their homes by a group of deserters from the Confederate Army, a breakaway band from the renegades led by William Quantrill.

Now, as Jack watched his aunt walk towards him he hardly recognized her. Gone was the spring in her step, the friendly wave to everybody she passed; the cheeky aside to every young cowboy who looked her way.

This was an old woman approaching. Jack rose from his perch on the house steps and went to meet her. He called her name in a greeting that stopped her in mid-stride. For several moments she stood staring silently at her young nephew as if she could hardly believe her ears or her eyes.

'Jack? Jack Crawford? Well God love us!'

Jack smiled at the look of surprise on his aunt's lined, sun-hardened face.

'That's right, Aunt Alice. It is me.'

Suddenly her features cracked into a smile.

'Jack Crawford!' she repeated. 'And here's us all believing you've been dead these last years.'

* * *

The parlour of Ma Bailey's guest house was much as Jack remembered it. A highly polished dining table with four chairs took pride of place in the centre of the room and two well-padded armchairs stood either side of an impressive fireplace.

A picture of Alice's late husband adorned the top of a low cabinet, which was flanked by two more soft chairs. A flowered carpet covered most of the floor and there was a large painting of a riverboat on one wall.

Jack and his aunt occupied the two armchairs in front of the unlit fire grate. Between them was a low table containing a coffee pot and china cups. The only blemish that Jack could see was the moose head above the mantel.

'You have to forgive young Tommy,' Alice said, explaining the sour greeting the young man had offered. 'He has no reason to love the name of Crawford. His folks ran the hardware store until they were forced to sell up by Clay and his partner. I keep him on to earn a few bucks to help the family finances. Times are tough for the Carters right now.'

Jack nodded. Even in the two hours or so he had been back in Creek Forks he had got the impression that things were tough for a lot of people around town.

He leaned forward, rested his elbows on his knees and steepled his fingertips in front of his face. His coffee remained untouched while he digested more news that his aunt had delivered moments earlier.

'You say that it was my brother who told you I had been killed?' he said, hardly able to keep the disbelief out of his voice.

'That's right, son,' Alice confirmed. 'It wasn't too long after — ' she paused ' — after your parents were killed. Clay was in town and he was drunk. Angry and very drunk. He was cussing and drinking heavy, got himself into a fight over some news from the war. He started yelling about the war being a waste of time and money and that it had cost him his parents and a young brother. 'Crazy young fool had to go off and fight just to prove he was a man. Getting himself killed for nothing.' That's how he made it to be.'

There was a silence between them. Jack was well aware that the war had destroyed many things — family lives, communities, even states — and brought major disruption to communications. He remembered how it had sometimes taken weeks for his pay to arrive, so how could Clay have learned that his young brother had been killed, even when it was untrue?

Jack would have a night's rest at the guest house before taking a ride out to the family ranch on the west of town beyond where the creek split, a landmark that had given the community its name.

He was about to let the matter rest when Alice Bailey suddenly said: 'You'll see a lot of changes around town since you lived out this way, Jack.'

He nodded. 'I've already noticed. People seem so . . . depressed.'

Alice slumped back into the chair opposite him.

'That's about it, son. Depressed. Businesses have been shut down; some folks have given up their homes and moved out. You'll have passed the boarded stores on your way here from the stage depot. And now — ' she paused ' — my store is being closed. I have just been to the bank to get myself a loan to see me through these dark times. I was wasting my breath.'

Jack gave his aunt a puzzled look. 'I don't understand. You mean old George Olsen won't offer you a loan? He's been a family friend for years. He knows you're good for the money.'

His aunt snorted.

'George would have been fine, except he's not around these days. Like I said things are different now and one thing you didn't notice on your way here. It's now Bannon's Bank.'

There was another short silence before Jack asked: 'What's happened, Alice? And who's this Bannon?'

'I reckon there's only one man who can answer that for you. I know Clay is your brother — he's family to me too, remember — but I think if you are planning to pay him a visit you'd best be ready for one of those changes.'

3

Clayton Crawford had two visitors, one of them a round-faced man in a brown checked suit who had arrived in town the day before.

Frederick Tibbs had come armed with documents, legal books and a certificate that confirmed he was an attorney in Springfield, Missouri. The paperwork would be more than enough to convince the local farmers and store owners that it would be in their best interests to sell up and move out. All legal and correct. That the land they farmed was not theirs.

The other visitor to the Circle-C was Vic Bannon.

Friendly negotiation to move out the farmers and homesteaders would have been Clay's first option. But he had others. And between them they had the men to carry them out. Vic Bannon owed him plenty. Hadn't he just helped to get the old man's kid off a murder charge?

'This place is sure off the old beaten tracks,' said Tibbs sipping his third whiskey.

'Not for long, Tibbs, not for long. But then you won't hear of it as Creek Forks. Crawford City sounds a whole lot better than that, don't you think?'

Tibbs finished his drink. He had met Clay Crawford only twice before but he was enough of a judge of character to recognize a power-hungry man when he saw one. And with a man like Vic Bannon pulling his strings nothing could go wrong.

He had made his own inquiries and discovered that the Crawford family had been important folk around this backwater Missouri town until the parents were butchered by a group of Quantrill's Raiders just a few days after the same men had plundered and torched the Kansas town of Lawrence in '63.

Crawford had declared a war on all things military, especially those in grey jackets. And they, Tibbs discovered, included his own brother. Now he was gathering his own forces to control the southwest corner of the county. It was a bold plan and Tibbs had not needed much convincing to become part of it.

Clay was a big man in stature — six three and two hundred and thirty pounds — and big on ambition. So much so that he had not hesitated to squash the one person who might have raised enough support to stand in his way. The fact that she was his dead father's sister had not caused him a moment's conscience. If Crawford was to be the powerhouse of Creek Forks he could not allow the likes of Alice Bailey to stand in his way.

He had to be ruthless, which was why he had persuaded Vic Bannon to order his bank manager to refuse her the loan she needed to keep her general store in operation. He had already claimed her small chicken farm on the pretence of helping out. A loan, followed by a reminder of the conditions of the loan, a few words of encouragement and then quiet but firm threats. Now, only by putting up that lucrative guest house as surety would she be granted a bank loan. And she would never do that. Her spirits were already close to be being broken and once she had given up her store it would be a signal to the rest of the people that Creek Forks was now Crawford territory. The farmers who had stubbornly refused to leave would find that there were other ways to get them off the rich grazing lands of the valley — far less pleasant than even the derisory token price that Crawford and Bannon, via this Springfield lawyer, would offer.

Bannon may have been the money man behind this scheme but Clay Crawford believed he was the brains.

However, Tibbs had just one more card to play before he agreed to become a silent partner in the Crawford empire-building. He glanced across at the third man, noticed Bannon's almost imperceptible nod, poured himself another whiskey and said: 'You haven't mentioned the second half of my fee.'

Clay smiled — a rarity these past four years. 'I haven't forgotten, Tibbs. It is time that Creek Forks had a new mayor to keep the locals under control.'

'Mayor Tibbs. Sounds fine to me,' said the man from Springfield, 'and with a lawyer's practice to go with it.'

Ben Lockhart, who had been the town's mayor for as long as Clay could remember, may have been a pain in the ass with all his town ordnances and council meetings but he had his uses. He managed to keep Clay just the right side of the law but Tibbs could probably do just as much.

The lawyer raised his glass and emptied it of its contents.

'Here's to you, Mr Crawford,' he said, his voice a slight slur.

He was far too concerned with his own self-congratulations to notice the sneer that crossed Crawford's face.

Once Frederick Tibbs had outlived his usefulness Clay would have other plans for him and they did not include the position of Mayor of Crawford City.

And the same went for the other man in the room. Vic Bannon was a means to an end.

*   *   *

Jack Crawford slept soundly in a comfortable bed and for the first time in two years, felt no pain from his wounds. He rose early on the morning of the first full day back in his home town.

Ahead of him was a visit to his brother and from what his aunt had told him it was unlikely to be a friendly reunion. Clay believed his young brother had been killed in the war and the news had hardly been greeted with an outpouring of sorrow at the loss.

But had Clay changed so much? It was natural that their parents' death had hit him hard but maybe his brother's 'resurrection' would turn out to be the jolt he needed to show him the error of the path he had taken.

'Don't expect too much,' Alice had warned him before he retired the previous night. 'This is not the Clay you remember. When your folks were killed, the ranch was in a bad way and he went into partnership with a man called Vic Bannon. You won't know the Bannons, Vic and his son Blake. They came towards the end of the war and bought up the old Lassiter place that backed on to the Circle-C. They tried to buy out Clay but your brother had the ace — the water that flows east of town through your place and on to the Lassiter spread — but you know all that.

'It seems Clay and Vic Bannon got on well and came to an agreement. Link the Circle-C with the Lassiters' Lazy-L; rebuild the old ranch house that had been burned out during the raid. There's even been talk among the farmers that Bannon and your brother plan to dam the creek to cut off the other small ranchers.'

'So, the Circle-C is no longer a real Crawford ranch?'

'It is hardly even the Circle-C any more, it's a big rambling place and if you want my opinion Clay and Bannon have only just started.

'When my own place ran into trouble, Clay was quick to offer his help but when things got worse he was just as quick to call in the debt. I had no choice but to let him take over my place next to the Lassiters'. He closed it down, killed the stock, and that left my general store in trouble.

'Bannon owns the bank but I don't doubt that it was Clay who made sure I didn't get a loan unless I put this place up as collateral. If he can do that to family, then God help the rest of the town.'

Jack got out of his comfortable bed, dressed in a clean shirt and pants and pulled his leather wallet from his luggage bag. His eighty dollars a month pay as a second lieutenant in the Confederate Army had remained untouched during his years of recuperation and this, with other savings, had left him, if not exactly rich, financially sound — enough, he figured, to see his aunt through to better times. He was anxious about seeing his brother again, but he could no longer put off a visit out to what had been the family home and ranch and was now, in the words of Alice Bailey, a big, rambling place with no name.

He picked up his walking cane, and studied it before tossing it to one side. There was a time to stand again on his own two feet and there was no better time than right now. As he made his way along the sidewalk towards the livery stable where he knew he could buy himself a horse, the limp was less noticeable.

Jack Crawford's new life was about to begin.

* * *

Clay Crawford stood on the veranda and watched Frederick Tibbs drive his buggy away from the ranch and out towards the narrow bridge that crossed the creek and linked the spread to the town.

To the north, what had been the Lassiter ranch was now Bannon-owned while nestled on the rich land where the small river forked was Alice Bailey's farm. To the south of her place more homesteaders were his target and then there was the Dutchman's to the west. Beyond that was open country which, with Tibbs's connivance and Bannon's hired guns, would become part of the new Crawford County.

Clay reckoned that two years — three at the most — would be needed before he would be powerful enough to earn a place in the state legislature as the richest man in the territory.

He threw down a half-finished cigar and went back inside the ranch house. With Tibbs and Bannon now out of the way he had unfinished business upstairs in the bedroom where the woman would be eagerly preparing herself for his return. At least she would be if she knew what was good for her.

Jack picked out a chestnut from Lee Dillon's stable and got a bit more information to go with it. Dillon had been a close friend of Billy Crawford and he was the first person, other than Alice to greet Jack's return to Creek Forks with a friendly smile.

'It's good to see the bad news wasn't true, young Jack. We all heard you were killed somewhere down south.'

'Shot up a bit,' Jack confirmed, 'but even us rebs had good doctors so I got through it. How's things here, Lee?'

The smile faded.

'You could be my last sale, son. I'm moving out at the end of the week.'

'You're another one who has sold up?'

'You could call it that — except I've

almost given the place away. To Vic Bannon. You won't know him — he came after you left. He's teamed up with Clay and it looks like they are aiming to buy up the whole territory at rock bottom prices. Bannon owns the bank, the old Lassiter place and now my horse trading business.'

'And Clay's got Aunt Alice's small farm,' Jack offered.

Dillon went on to repeat what Jack had quickly discovered from his aunt on his first night back and when he left the stable with a firm handshake and a less than enthusiastic, 'Give my regards to your brother,' Jack was aware of a growing tension at what lay ahead.

He attempted to lighten the mood by asking about Dillon's daughter. He had known Lucy since they were both young children and she had been a bubbly, friendly girl during all her teen years. She was one of the few people he felt he would genuinely miss during his stay in the army — one he would look forward to seeing again when the war was over.

But his question did not bring the answer he was hoping to hear.

'Best ask your brother about her, Jack. She's been taking up with him this last year. Her ma and me don't see much of her these days.'

There was a deep sadness in the stableman's voice when they shook hands.

As he headed out of town, Jack passed a buggy driven by the brown-suited man who had been a fellow stage passenger they day before. They nodded an unspoken greeting and went their separate ways.

★　★　★

The reunion was as unbrotherly as Jack had been led to believe it would be. The Circle-C sign had been removed from its pride of place above the ranch gates and the house, less than half a mile further along the road, was an unfamiliar sight, completely rebuilt after the raid four years earlier. It was a big two-storey building that stretched to where the old barn had been; the barn where Jack and his brother had enjoyed long hours of boyhood adventures was no longer there.

Jack dismounted, tethered his horse to a hitching rail — one thing that was a reminder of the old days — and climbed the steps into the house.

Inside was a vast room, impressively and expensively furnished with a wide, shining oak table, and cabinets filled with glassware and trophies. An array of historic weapons in glass cases hung on the walls while a huge window opened out on to a wide expanse of greenery, which Jack remembered with great affection. Off to the left a winding staircase led up to a balcony and presumably, bedrooms and living quarters. A half-opened door to the right revealed the kitchen of the house.

Jack removed his hat and surveyed

the scene, a far different picture from the one he remembered. Even the old sideboard that had been the home for family pictures was no longer there.

There was no sign of life. Jack called out his brother's name.

No reply.

He tried again. 'Clay! Are you home?'

Suddenly, a door at the top of the staircase opened and Clay Crawford staggered into view. He was in a state of undress and was clearly drunk. He leaned on the railing and peered down at his visitor.

'Who's there?'

Jack walked to the foot of the staircase but before he could go any further the door of the room re-opened and the half-naked figure of Lucy Dillon appeared at Clay's shoulder.

Lucy's voice was almost a screech of excitement.

'Jack! Clay, it's your brother!'

There was no rush down the staircase to greet a brother back from the dead. Instead, Clay stood holding the rail to stop himself from swaying.

'Well, ain't that right? My war hero brother ain't dead after all, even though he picked to fight on the losing side. The loser returns.'

Jack stayed at the foot of the stairs.

'Looks like I picked a bad time to come calling, Clay.'

'What makes you think there's ever gonna be a good time, brother? You ran out on your folks, including me, your big brother, to fight for a bunch of rebels. The sort of men who killed our parents, who burned our place down, so, no there won't be a good time to come calling.'

Jack looked around and studied the room more closely. This was a room of a man with money.

'Looks like you didn't do too bad out of it, Clay,' Jack snapped. 'You got the ranch and looks to me like you've got the girl.'

There was going to be no reunion this day. Or maybe any day.

'So long, Clay. And Lucy. Oh, and

your father asked me to say hello for him before he sells up and moves on.'

The girl shook herself free from Clay's grip, made an attempt at modesty by wrapping the flowing robe around her nakedness and raced along the landing and down the stairs.

'Stop, Jack! Wait!'

But he did not stop. Instead he increased his pace and hurried outside. This was no place for him. Alice had been right. Clay was a changed man — not the brother he had left behind five years ago. The break of the family ties was complete. The war had claimed another victim two years after it ended.

⋆ ⋆ ⋆

Jack headed back to Ma Bailey's guest house in a state of deep depression. Not only had his meeting with Clay gone badly wrong, the sight of Lucy Dillon rushing half-naked down the stairs caused him to think that Creek Forks was not the place for him.

Perhaps he should have stayed and listened to what Lucy wanted to say. He hadn't given her a chance, just like Clay hadn't given him a chance.

He made a short stop at Lee Dillon's stable to tell him that he had spoken to Lucy and she was fine — a small deception that he felt was justified. There was no reason to add to the man's problems.

Jack tethered his horse outside his aunt's place and went into the house to discover that she had a visitor, an old family friend, Ben Lockhart, the mayor of Creek Forks.

He greeted Jack with a firm handshake and the smile of a man who was genuinely pleased to see him.

'Alice has been telling me all about what happened to you,' said Lockhart. 'Got to say, young Jack, you've really cheered up the old girl here by turning up like you did.'

'Glad to help,' Jack grinned.

'She tells me you've been out to the

old place to see your brother. How was it?'

'Not good,' Jack answered, sliding into a chair opposite the mayor. 'I reckon Clay's changed a lot since I saw him.'

'Since your folks were killed and he teamed up with the Bannons he's not been the same,' Lockhart agreed.

'He's gone bad,' Alice snapped. 'There is no way of saying it different. He's hell bent on taking over the town, him and Bannon, and he isn't going to let anybody get in his way. Not even family.'

Jack felt no inclination to come to his brother's defence. What he had seen had been enough to confirm what Alice and Lockhart were saying about him. Lee Dillon had expressed the same opinion.

'What are your own plans?' the mayor asked suddenly.

Jack shrugged.

'Nothing's settled. I haven't spoken to Alice yet, but — ' he looked across at his aunt ' — I'd like to help her get the store up and running again.'

'That's good of you, Jack, but the bank's turned me down unless I put this place up as collateral. I'm not doing that, so I'm selling out.'

Jack reached out and grasped her hand.

'Don't worry about the bank. I've got money doing nothing. We can stock up from the other farmers. I can get a job. We'll be fine.'

Alice opened her mouth to protest but it was Lockhart who silenced her.

'It's worth listening, Ma. Jack's making a good offer.'

'What kind of job could you do, Jack?' she protested feebly. 'You've got that leg wound — '

'We'll be fine,' he repeated. 'The leg's improving all the time. I'll soon be able to throw that cane away. Aunt Alice, you worry too much.'

Reluctantly, Alice Bailey nodded. 'Well, the least I can do is give you the room for as long as you need it.'

They hugged their agreement and the mayor added his approval with a warm handshake.

★   ★   ★

Ben Lockhart strode across the street to the Flag Hotel, as he still called the Aces High. That was where he expected to find Luke Franklin. He was not disappointed, the Creek Forks lawman was in his usual seat at a corner table staring into an empty whiskey glass.

Lockhart slipped into a vacant chair and leaned across to refill Franklin's glass from the bottle in the middle of the table.

'Think you're going to find answers in a bottle, Sheriff? Go ahead.'

Franklin snatched up the glass.

'Leave me alone, Mayor. Can't a man have a drink in peace?'

'You're not just any man, Luke, You're the sheriff of this town.' Lockhart tried to keep his anger under control. 'And right now I've just left a meeting of the town councillors who want me to give you a message.'

Franklin snorted. 'And what did that bunch of old scuttlebutts want you to tell me?'

'They want your star.'

The sheriff paused with the refilled glass only half way to his lips. He slammed it down with a bang, suddenly very sober.

'You can't take that,' he smirked. 'Crawford and Bannon won't let it happen.'

Lockhart remained calm.

'Let me remind you, Luke, you're employed by the town, not Clay Crawford or Vic Bannon. And right now, you're not doing the job you're being paid for. Take a look at yourself: a drunk with a badge and a gun.

'We all know you think Bannon will keep you in office after what you did for that no-good son of his. And if he don't there's always Crawford — what's he paying you, Luke? I hope he's getting his money's worth.'

'Now wait a minute, Mayor. Nobody saw Blake shoot that Thomas kid. I couldn't lock him up,' Franklin protested.

'You made no effort to find out what happened. Lester was only a boy.'

'He was a thief and even if young Bannon had killed him, without witnesses he would have walked free.'

Lockhart grunted. 'That's not for you to decide, Luke.' Then in a more conciliatory tone, he went on: 'You've been sheriff here for a long time and we appreciate what you have done to keep this town peaceful, but it's time for you — and the town — to move on. It's time for a younger man to take some of the burden.'

He paused for effect before adding: 'I talked the council into letting you stay, but there's a condition.'

Franklin drank his whiskey and waited.

'This town — and that means you — need a deputy sheriff, somebody who is ready to step up when the time comes for you to retire.'

Luke Franklin smiled, a rarity since he began his own soul-searching following the immediate release of Blake Bannon.

'And who are you going to find in this town who'll take on the job? Forty dollars a month ain't going to get you a man worth the name.'

'Leave that to us, Luke. Meantime, cut down on the whiskey or I won't be able to hold off the rest of the councillors much longer.'

Lockhart rose from the table and left the saloon. Outside, he breathed heavily, expanding his chest in a gesture that signified satisfaction. He had taken the first step towards loosening the growing stranglehold of fear Clay Crawford and Vic Bannon were building.

The next step would be to face the man he felt would be perfect for the job.

4

Caleb Jones leaned on his plough, wiped the sweat from his face and gazed out at the rolling hills. It was hot work on a hot day and made even hotter by a growing anger, not an emotion that regularly afflicted the 50-year-old Kentuckian.

He had farmed the southwest creek area for most of his adult life and he was not about to throw it all away by handing over to men like Clay Crawford and Vic Bannon at a price of their choosing. He had known Crawford a lot of years and their sons had been close friends, but things were different now. His son Jos had been one of the hundreds of thousands of young men who had given their lives for a cause. His wife was little more than a shadow of the woman she was.

Alice Bailey had already sold out and

others of his neighbours like Felix Sykes and Dan Curtis were thinking about it. Caleb had called a meeting at his place where he hoped to convince the other valley farmers that they should all stick together.

He gazed out towards the hilltop to the east. He had visitors, two riders silhouetted against the clear sky. They began their approach down the slope but they appeared to be in no hurry to reach him.

They were still two hundred yards away when he recognized the man on the right. Blake Bannon was a tall, slim figure in a red shirt and black vest. He rode a white stallion and, as Caleb knew from experience, was a sour-faced spoiled kid who had inherited a mean streak from his father. His companion, shorter, running to fat, Caleb knew only by name. Zeke Emmett had come to Creek Forks along with the Bannons and was just another of the hired hoodlums on the payroll.

They pulled their horses to a stop

alongside Caleb's plough. Bannon leaned forward in his saddle but neither man made any move to dismount.

'You look all done in, Caleb,' Bannon said, making a feeble effort to smile. 'Aren't you getting a bit old for this sort of work?'

'What do you want, Bannon? I'm busy.'

'Hey, now that's no way to greet a friendly neighbour making a social call.'

He turned to Emmett. 'Don't that strike you a mite unfriendly, Zeke?'

'It sure does,' Emmett smirked. 'Not neighbourly at all.'

'Like I said, Bannon, what do you want?' Caleb said defiantly.

'Well, since you ain't in the mood to make social talk, I hear you've got yourself a meeting coming up. You and the rest of the farmers.'

'You hear right. So what? Not that it is any of your business.'

'Just a bit of friendly advice, Caleb. The old man has made you and your small-time farmer friends good offers for your land. When you go to your meeting, I'd advise you to suggest to them that they take up those offers. Things could get really tough for you around here if you don't.'

'Is that a threat?'

Blake Bannon grinned. 'Like I say, just a bit of friendly advice.'

'Well, here's some back for you, messenger boy. Tell your old man and that snake of a partner of his, Clay Crawford, that I won't be selling, no matter what he offers. I'm staying. So get off my land and take that pet pup with you.'

Blake Bannon swung his horse round and led it across to where Emmett had stopped.

'You hear that, Zeke? Is that what you are, a pet pup?'

'And you a messenger boy.'

'I don't think our neighbour's got the message, do you?'

The two men dismounted and Caleb knew that the talking was over and that he was in big trouble. Twenty years younger, he would gladly have stood toe to toe with this pair but the way Emmett pulled on his black gloves and the menace in Bannon's eyes provided a clear enough warning of what was to come.

He looked around for something — anything — he could use to defend himself. Anything for protection. The nearest thing, a loose log, was out of reach. He braced himself for the attack as Emmett thudded his right fist into his left palm.

Caleb was giving both men more than twenty years in age and several pounds in weight but he was not going to go down without a fight.

He crouched in readiness for the attack but he was not prepared for what happened next. By keeping a close watch on Emmett he had not noticed Blake emerging from behind his horse armed with a bullwhip. Without warning he suddenly felt the lash across his shoulder, ripping his shirt and drawing blood. Bannon screeched a yell of triumph and repeated the treatment, this time catching Caleb around the throat and dragging him forward.

The farmer fell face first into the dust and as he tried to get to his feet he found himself looking up at the leering face of Blake Bannon. There was hate in the young man's eyes as he drew back his fist and smashed it into Caleb's jaw.

The older man scrambled in the dirt and blind fury engulfed him. He knew this could become a fight to the death — the others were both armed — but desperation overcame fear as he launched himself at Bannon, hurling fistfuls of dust into the other's eyes. The pair hit the ground with a sickening thud and for a brief moment Caleb thought he had knocked the wind from Bannon's body. But before he could take any advantage, a fierce smash from a gun butt sent a searing pain through his back and this was followed by a brutal kick to the stomach, which forced him to curl into a ball in a futile attempt at self-protection.

Another kick . . . then another.

He closed his eyes and then waited for the next blow. But none came. Instead, when he opened his eyes, it was to discover that his two assailants had remounted. Bannon was staring down at him.

'Now, Caleb, I have tried being real neighbourly but it seems you ain't interested in that. Tomorrow, you'll be getting a visit from a Mister Tibbs, a lawyer in from Springfield. He will have with him a bill of sale for this hole in the ground you call a farm. You'll sign that bill of sale and tonight you'll tell your meeting that is what you're going to do. And you'll tell the rest of those sodbusters to do the same.'

He turned his stallion, spat viciously at the stricken farmer and the two men headed back the way they had come.

Caleb struggled to his feet, clutching his stomach and retching as he tried to cling on to his plough for balance. Delicately, he touched his bleeding lip and bruised face, his left eye slowly closing as the swelling increased on his face.

Caleb Jones was a broken man.

* * *

Jack had known Luke Franklin since he was a child and he could never claim to have liked the man. Now the thought of working alongside him as his deputy was not the most appealing suggestion he had ever heard.

'It's a job and the pay may not be good but at least it's a start in getting your life back together,' his aunt stressed when Ben Lockhart put the idea to both of them.

'And I reckon it will not be too long before you are sheriff of this town,' the mayor said. 'Luke is nearing the end of the line. He's drinking too much and he's neglecting the job.'

'It sounds to me like you want

somebody in there to spy on him,' Jack answered.

Lockhart smiled. 'Maybe that, too, young feller. What do you say?'

'Well, like Alice said, it's a job and that's what I need at the moment. But what does Franklin think about this?'

'You let me worry about Luke,' the mayor said, now sure that he had hooked himself a young deputy, and an honest man. Even so, he felt duty bound to give one word of warning to the prospective new lawman.

'It may mean you will run into Clay from time to time. By run into, I mean legally. There are folks around here who think your brother's association with the Bannons is not just about building himself a cattle empire.'

The prospect of crossing swords with his brother held no fears for Jack. His one visit to the old Circle-C had been enough to convince him that Clay had made a new life for himself, and it did not include Jack.

The mayor continued: 'Creek Forks

won't be off the beaten track if the new West Tennessee Railroad company get to finish their plans to run a link up through to Independence and Kansas City. This will be a major trading centre and a rich cattle town.

'What we have that all cattle need, Jack, is water . . . rivers of the stuff. Clay and Bannon are hell bent on buying up all the land around those rivers and when the thousands of heads of beef come this way, who will the trail bosses and owners be paying for water?' He paused before adding: 'We think that the people of Creek Forks should share in what riches that will bring . . . but that doesn't seem to be part of Clay's plans.'

Jack smiled. 'So, I've been warned,' he said, rising from the table to lean over and shake hands with Lockhart.

'Sounds like I'll have to get myself a gun.'

'I'm sure the town can afford to pay for one of those,' Lockhart said.

'I'm sure, too, Mayor, but what I was

about to say was that I hope I'll never have to use it. I'd be more than happy if it turned out to be the last gun in Creek Forks.'

* * *

Jenny Lang gathered the empty dinner plates and smiled at the two people who had greeted her at the stage depot and were now providing her with a new home for as long as she needed it. Her aunt and uncle — Bessie and Felix Sykes — were delighted to have their niece as the new school teacher and now she was repaying their hospitality by cooking for them and cleaning their small farm house.

Bessie Sykes was a sickly woman. She had trouble with her breathing and Jenny had already heard her night time coughing was keeping her awake for hours. Her uncle Felix looked a lot older than she remembered, though it had been less than three years since they visited her and her family in

Wichita, Kansas.

'Apple pie, Uncle?' she asked, knowing the answer would be a grin of satisfaction. Bessie silently waved away the offer. She had not been eating well for some time.

'She's very worried,' Felix had confided the previous evening when Jenny and her uncle were taking a walk around the grounds outside the house. 'We've been offered money to sell up and move out. We don't think it is a good offer but with your aunt's health in such a poor state we may have no choice. The doctor has told her that the drier air out West, Colorado maybe, would be helpful but I am sure it would break her heart if we had to move far away.'

Jenny listened while he told her of the new men in the district, Vic Bannon and his son Blake who had joined forces with Clay Crawford to buy out all the small farmers.

'And if we won't sell, he's made no secret of the fact that he would make life very uncomfortable for all of us.'

It was at the mention of the Crawford name that Jenny's interest increased.

'I came in on the stage with a young man of that name. Jack Crawford — he seemed like a pleasant enough person.'

Felix Sykes stopped in mid-stride.

'Jack? We all thought he had been killed in the war. Now you say he's still alive?'

'Wounded — he walks with a cane — but very much alive. The sad thing is he only learned from the man at Jackson's Trading Post where we sheltered from the storm that his parents had been killed.'

Felix shook his head. 'I wish I had seen him getting off the stage. Maybe I was too taken with you arriving. 'It was a terrible business, my dear. Really bad. Raiders burned the ranch house down, killed the folks, except for Clay, Jack's older brother.'

They had walked along in silence for several minutes before Felix said: 'It sounds as though you met the nicer of the Crawford brothers, young lady. I wonder if I am going to have to keep a close eye on you.'

Jenny blushed at the thought but there was a hint of truth in her uncle's assumption. She had taken an instant liking to the young soldier, even though he had been in the Confederate Army. The war was over; people had to learn to live together. She thought the time was not far away before she tried to learn a bit more about handsome Jack Crawford.

★ ★ ★

The meeting in Caleb Jones's barn was going just as he had expected. The farmers were losing their will to fight.

'Look at you, Caleb,' Dan Curtis said, waving his hands in the air. 'Bruised and beaten, without half your teeth and whipped by some hot head. Booted in the gut by that no-good kid and his sidekick and you want to stick it out! Why? Life's gonna be hell around these parts if Crawford and Bannon don't get what they want. I've got a wife and three young 'uns to support. Maybe we should all think about taking the money and getting out.'

'Now, hold on a minute, Dan.' It was another neighbour, a strong-willed Dutchman named Lars Akerman who interrupted. 'Caleb isn't saying that. According to Bannon we'll be getting a visit from some big shot lawyer with an offer — '

'Not an offer!' Curtis snapped. 'A bill of sale. That's what he said, ain't it, Caleb?'

The injured man nodded.

'So we don't even get a chance to say how much our land is worth,' Felix Sykes put in. 'Bannon makes it sound like a deal is already done.'

'Unless we all want some of what Caleb's had,' Curtis said. 'I'm for selling up but if Caleb won't move, my place won't be worth a dime. It's too far from the creek to be of any value to

Crawford or Bannon or anybody without Caleb's place.'

Will Horn, one of the older group of homesteaders, got to his feet.

'Can't our town sheriff do something about all this? It's the sort of trouble we pay him to sort out.'

'We pay him so he can get drunk all day,' Akerman said. 'Besides, he's in Crawford's debt up to his neck, all the time he spends in that casino. He does exactly as he's told.'

'How about the mayor?' one of the others, Frank Miller, suggested. 'He has always seemed to me to be a decent man.'

'Lockhart's a good enough man but he doesn't have any real power. As for our esteemed town councillors, well . . . '

There was a murmur of agreement from all around the barn.

Felix Sykes looked around at the faces; there was despair on most of them, fear in some but in the bruised and bloodied features of Caleb Jones he saw defiance. He knew, though, that the resolve of one man would not be enough to save the valley from the clutches of Clay Crawford and the Bannons.

He got to his feet. 'I think we should all meet back here at noon tomorrow and when this lawyer comes calling we listen to what he has to say.'

'We know what he's gonna say,' Caleb growled.

'Even so,' Felix said quietly, 'we all ought to hear it before we decide what's best to do.'

'We have to stick together,' Dan Curtis barked. 'Whatever we decide has to be the best for us all. Like I said, without Caleb's place, the rest is no good to them.'

Horn stood up to have his say. 'I agree with Felix. We hear what this lawyer's offering and then decide. I'm too old to be fighting some kind of range war but I sure as hell ain't for giving my place away. They'll have to bury me under it first.'

'They may do just that,' a grim-faced Curtis said sourly. 'But that goes for all of us.'

The meeting of farmers and homesteaders broke up with an agreement to be back at noon the next day to face the man from Springfield.

★   ★   ★

Luke Franklin was aching for a drink but he knew it would have to wait. He had just witnessed Jack Crawford being sworn in as town deputy and listened to the mayor's pompous description of the ex-soldier's duties.

Luke knew better than to believe a word of it. Young Crawford was there for one reason only: to spy on him. Well, he would soon solve that problem. Clay Crawford would not take kindly to the news that his younger brother was now a lawman.

Reluctantly, he shook hands with his new deputy, pointed out his desk and then gave his first order.

'I have to make a call, so I'll leave you to man the office for an hour or two,' he said, then he picked his hat off its hook and followed Mayor Lockhart out into the heat of the morning sun.

Jack allowed himself a private smile. The sheriff's cool handshake and his stony-faced acceptance of his new deputy had confirmed his belief that he was not the most welcome visitor to the small office at the corner of Main and South streets.

He settled himself in a chair and studied his new surroundings. The usual wanted bills covered the wall at the side of the door and there was a tall cabinet to his left. A door to the right of the cabinet led to two cells, regularly occupied by drunks thrown out of the Aces High Casino Bar or any other of Creek Forks' three saloons.

Jack slid open the left hand drawer of his new desk. It was empty. He tried the drawer on the right. It was jammed.

Or locked.

A ring of keys hung on a hook beside

the entrance to the cells but after three attempts to open the drawer, it was clear that none of them fitted the lock. After searching the desk for another key he gave up. Whatever Franklin had locked away would still be there later.

Across the street, Sheriff Franklin was already on his second drink of the day. He needed a third to give him the courage to face Clay Crawford. What he had to say to his boss could not wait.

* * *

Frederick Tibbs was not alone when he arrived at Caleb Jones's place. Four riders flanked his buggy as he drew it to a halt outside the small house that had been Caleb's home for more than twenty years.

But Caleb too was not alone. He had friends around him to meet the lawyer who had come to take his home away from him.

They all knew that this was not going to be a friendly meeting.

Tibbs climbed down from his buggy but the four men who had escorted him remained in their saddles. Caleb studied them. Blake Bannon was not there but the man he had called a pet pup — Zeke Emmett — was. And he was smirking.

He had never seen any of the others before but he had no doubt that they were little more than hired guns working for Clay Crawford, Vic Bannon — or both. But Caleb had his own support. The rest of the farmers stood at his shoulder as Tibbs approached.

Caleb thought the lawyer looked nervous. He was sweating profusely even though it was a cool morning. Tibbs looked anxiously around, as if trying to assure himself that his escorts were on hand in the case of any trouble.

'Mr Jones,' he said, stretching out his hand. 'I am Frederick Tibbs.'

Caleb ignored the offer of a handshake.

'I know who you are, mister. We just want to hear what you have to say.'

Tibbs coughed. 'This is a private matter, Mr Jones. Should we not go inside?'

Caleb snorted his reply.

'What you've got to say affects all of us. They all want to know what Crawford and Bannon are offering for my place. Then they'll know what to expect.'

There were mutterings of agreement from the group who had gathered at the Jones place.

'Very well,' Tibbs agreed. He reached inside his coat pocket and produced a document, which he offered to Caleb.

'I'm here on behalf of Mr Clayton Crawford to offer you the sum of two thousand dollars — '

He got no further. Caleb snatched the paper from his hand and shook it violently in front of the lawyer's face.

'Two thousand dollars? Let me tell you, Mr Fancy Lawyer, you can get right back in that buggy and get on back to Clay Crawford, taking your hounds with you and you can tell him that Caleb Jones and his friends ain't for sale.'

'And that goes for the rest of us!' the Dutchman led the shouts of agreement from the other farmers.

Frederick Tibbs remained unmoved.

'Mr Jones,' he said, his voice even, his manner unchanged. 'You don't seem to understand. That would be very unwise. Mr Crawford has made you a generous offer as a token of goodwill — an offer he does not in law have to make. It's an offer to you,' he turned and faced the others, 'and to all of you.

'I am here from my office in Springfield as his legal representative and it is my duty to tell you that I have lodged in the bank of that city documents that confirm you have no rights to this land, that under state law, Mr Crawford is only requested to pay for your property — building, farm equipment and furniture. It is up to the state to decide on actual ownership of the land and I can assure you that, in such a dispute Mr Crawford would be the man to take ownership. Believe me, gentlemen, the law of Missouri is on Mr Crawford's side.'

Silence fell over the gathering of farmers. It was broken only when Dan Curtis barked: 'That's got to be a filthy legal lie. Most of us have been farming this land for nearly twenty years, some even longer. You can't just come in and take away all we have worked for.'

Caleb reached forward and made a grab for Tibbs's shirt front but the fat man saw it coming and backed off quickly.

'That would be unwise, Mr Jones,' he said coolly. 'As you see, I have brought some of Mr Crawford's staff along with me as a protection against such aggressive behaviour.'

But Caleb would not be silenced.

'Then let me tell you this. You and your fancy legal talk and Crawford and Bannon with their gunslingers don't frighten us. If he wants us off our land he's going to have to move us with something a lot more impressive than some smart-talking city lawyer with his documents and fancy talk. If Crawford and Bannon want this land they're gonna have to fight to get it. And he will have to be ready to spill blood — maybe even their own.'

For the first time since his arrival, Frederick Tibbs felt he was on unsafe ground. Were these men serious? Would they really fight Crawford and Bannon and people like the four riders who had accompanied him? These were farmers, not gunmen. Surely they would see sense and sign the bills of sale he had in his pocket?

He mopped his brow and climbed aboard the buggy.

'I will pass on your message, Mr Jones, but I must warn you, Mr Crawford has employed me to bring a peaceful solution to this problem. I cannot be responsible for what will happen.'

*   *   *

At the same time that the lawyer and his hired help were calling on Caleb Jones, Deputy Sheriff Jack Crawford was also receiving a visitor.

Franklin had not yet returned from his latest 'business call', which Jack suspected included a lengthy visit to the Aces High, when the office door opened and his brother stepped in from the street.

He was smiling.

'Clay,' Jack said simply but he did not get to his feet.

'Hello, brother.' The elder Crawford strode forward and reached out across the desk. Bewildered at the apparent change in his brother's attitude, Jack took the outstretched hand.

'What brings you into town?'

Clay let his smile linger.

'I came to apologize, Jack. For what I said when you came calling. I was drunk.'

Jack pointed to a chair.

'You sure were, Clay. And you weren't a pretty sight.'

His brother held up his arms in mock surrender.

'I'm sorry. Real sorry. But it came as a shock to see my young brother standing there at the bottom of the stairs. Four years after — '

'After you had told everybody I had been killed,' Jack offered with more than a hint of scorn in his voice.

Clay sighed.

'Look, brother, I only passed on the message that reached me.'

'Reached you from where, Clay? Who told you I'd been killed?'

'Come on, Jack. It was a long time ago. Our folks had been butchered, you were fighting a losing war, the whole country was in a mess. There were reports every day of people being killed in massacres everywhere. I can't remember who told me.'

Jack studied his brother's face. He couldn't remember who had told him his brother had been killed in the war? That took some believing but he let it pass. There was nothing to be gained by cross-examination.

But any acceptance of Clay's apparent change of heart was conditional. He waited for Clay to tell him the real reason for his visit and he did not have to wait for long.

'What the hell are you doing sitting here behind a desk and wearing a deputy's badge?'

Jack smiled. 'It's a job, Clay, and I need a job.'

'Look, brother, I can see you are still sore at me — what with Lucy and all — '

'Lucy?'

'I know how you were sweet on her before you went away but . . . well, time moves on and she's with me now.'

'I saw that and I wish you both well.'

Clay chuckled. 'And I wish you could have made that sound as though you meant it.'

'I do mean it. Like you say, time moves on and things change. But that's not what you came here to tell me.'

Clay stood up and walked away from

the desk as if playing over in his mind what to say next. Then, turning back, he said: 'When Luke Franklin told me he was taking you on as deputy, I thought: good. A lawman in the family can't be a bad thing.'

'Glad you're pleased, Clay, but I wasn't looking for your approval. From what I hear from Alice you and the law haven't exactly been on the best of terms lately.'

'Alice said that, did she?' Clay smirked. 'She's a brave old lady, that's for sure. And stubborn, too.'

He went back to his chair and rested his elbows on Jack's desk.

Leaning forward he said: 'The truth is I helped her out when things were tough. When they got even tougher and she couldn't pay she offered to let me take over her little farm. It seemed a deal that was fair to both of us. What was so wrong about that?'

'Nothing,' Jack agreed, 'it seems like a perfect arrangement. If that's the way it was.'

'It was,' Clay said but Jack raised his hand.

'Except you killed off all the live-stock, which meant she had nowhere to turn to stock up her small store here in town. Now that store is in trouble she's been refused a bank loan unless she puts up her guest house as security for repayment. On your say-so, she tells me.'

Clay didn't answer at once. Instead, he leaned back in his chair, flicked a match to light a cheroot and blew smoke up at the ceiling.

'You make it sound fairly ruthless, Jack, but Alice knew what to expect. Business is business,' he said eventually.

'Even to the point of ruining the family?'

'Ah, Jack, you always had a soft spot for Aunt Alice. But things have changed since you left. Creek Forks isn't going to be a sleepy no-account town for much longer. It's going to grow — and grow fast. And the Crawford family are going to be part of it. People like Alice

Bailey were standing in the way of progress. If it hadn't been me who bought her out — or forced her out as she probably explained it to you — then it would have been somebody else, a big city money man who has no feelings for this part of Missouri.'

He paused.

'Look, Jack, you don't want to be sitting here doing Luke Franklin's dirty work while he drinks himself into a stupor every day. The man's a drunk and he'll kill himself within a year. Then what will you do?'

'Probably become town sheriff,' Jack smiled. 'Like I said, it's a job.'

'You don't need this kind of job. You've done your bit for this country . . . even though you did pick the wrong side. It's time to reap some reward. Come back to the ranch, join me and Vic and help to make this place a town that people throughout the state will have heard about.'

It was the first time Clay mentioned his partner and Jack let him carry on before he asked: 'Vic? Who's Vic?'

'My partner, Vic Bannon — I guess Alice must have mentioned him while she was spreading all this dirt about me.'

'She mentioned him, Clay. I just wanted to hear you tell me who he was and how you came to know him.'

Clay eyed his brother with suspicion. What was going on in his head? But he carried on. 'Vic and his son bought the Lassiter place just after the war and we got together to form a cattle owners' group.'

'A group or just you and Bannon?'

'To start with, yes. But there will be others soon.'

'And when you heard that there were plans to bring the railroad though Creek Forks you thought it would be a good idea to buy up the small farms and all the grazing land on both sides of the river. Is that the plan — drive out all the small farmers?'

Clay Crawford snorted. 'Sodbusters!

89

What can they offer this part of the county? A few vegetables, chickens, sheep . . . this is cattle country, Jack. Big cattle country.'

Jack got to his feet.

'Sorry, Clay. These 'sodbusters' as you call them have been here for as long as the Crawfords and some a lot longer. They are neighbours, they were friends of our parents and your friends before the war.

'I can't come back to the Circle-C, Clay, if that's what it's still called. I've got a job here and I aim to carry it out.'

Clay rose to his feet and stood across the desk from his brother. He was almost half a foot taller than Jack but he stared cold-eyed at the young deputy. Gone was the friendly smile he had brought with him into the office. Now his face was like a stone.

'I'm sorry, too, Jack, but maybe not as sorry as you will be. You see, brother, it's like this — you are either with us or against us. That's how it has got to be.'

'In that case, I guess we will be on opposite sides.'

He stood his ground while Clay turned and stormed out of the office, slamming the door behind him.

5

Like her husband, Mary-Anne Horn had lived all her fifty-six years in the Creek Forks valley. She expected to die there and to be buried in the small church cemetery on the outskirts of town. She had never wanted to leave. Until now.

She was not sleeping well at night. She was not eating enough. And she knew this had been brought upon her by what had been happening since the Bannons arrived and bought the Lassiter place.

Everybody — the Horns, the Sykes, Curtises, Caleb Jones, even the Dutchman — had tried to make the newcomers welcome and to include them in the social life, such as it was around Creek Forks. But their attempts at friendship and neighbourliness had been shunned, especially by the son.

Blake Bannon was a hothead, just like her own boy, who had long since left the valley. The last she had heard about Ricky had been almost a year ago, a letter from a lawyer up in Paducah, Kentucky telling her that her son had been arrested after a barroom brawl in which a man had died. Ricky Horn was one of three men who were standing trial for the killing. Since then, nothing.

'And nothing's just what we want to hear from him,' her husband had snapped at the time. 'He's no good, Annie, and he's no son of ours.'

Disowning a boy she had brought into the world did not come quite so easily to Mary-Anne Horn. She needed to know how he was. It was a mother's nature.

Tomorrow, she would try again to persuade Will that their son was not a lost cause; that they should be trying to find him, maybe even to bring him home.

But that was for tomorrow. Tonight she stared up at the ceiling while beside her, Will breathed evenly in a deep sleep. Outside a wind was getting up and there would be more rain before the morning.

*   *   *

There were four night riders, all with their faces hidden beneath black hoods. And all were carrying torches. At the front, Zeke Emmett waved the others to a halt at the top of the rise.

Overhead, storm clouds were gathering and the wind was strengthening but there was still enough moonlight to make out the small homestead in the valley below.

It was an hour after midnight and the Horns would be sleeping. Beneath the hood, Emmett grinned at the thought that this would be the last time that they would sleep in their own bed. He was under orders. No killing. Not this time. Just get them out of their beds, out of the house and then burn it to the ground. No killing.

At least, Emmett reckoned, he could eagerly look into the old folks' faces as they watched the flames — his flames — rip the heart out of the wooden shack that had been their home for more than thirty years. He could take his own pleasure in that. He turned towards the three other men with their faces hidden in the blackness of the hoods.

'Remember. Nobody talks. And the boss says no killing. He only wants them out of the place.'

The rest grunted their reluctant agreement. They had done this before, but they had never been told there was to be no killing.

Emmett carried on with his orders. 'When we get to the house, I'll fire a few shots in the air. That'll waken them up and bring them out. After that, you all know what to do. Get the horses out of the barn — there ain't no sense in frying dumb animals — and burn what's left.'

Again there was muttered agreement

and, satisfied that they would follow his orders, Emmett signalled them forward and they began the descent towards the unsuspecting couple sleeping soundly in their beds.

* * *

But Mary-Anne Horn was not in her bed. Still unable to sleep and kept awake as much by her own thoughts of her absent son as the increasing noise of the wind, she had pulled a coat over her night clothes and was standing at the window.

She saw them at the top of the rise, half-hidden by a cluster of bushes but still visible enough for her to make out three, maybe four riders. Behind her Will Horn was still sleeping soundly.

Moving away from the window, she hurried across to the bed and shook her husband.

'Will! Wake up, Will!' She shook him harder.

Stirring, Will Horn grunted a protest.

'What is it, woman?'

'I reckon we've got visitors. Look.' She pointed towards the window and Will climbed quickly out of bed. The four horsemen were approaching slowly.

'Nobody pays a friendly visit at this time of night,' Will said quietly. 'Pass me the rifle.'

'Will, you can't go out there.'

'Pass me the rifle, Annie. Hurry.'

Snatching the weapon from his wife's hands, Horn pulled open the door and stepped out on to the porch to the noise of gunfire and the sight of four hooded riders carrying flaming torches. It stopped him in his tracks but he was quick to recover.

'Hold it right there!' he shouted. 'Not one more step.'

The front rider fired into the sky. Then again. He remembered the instructions. No killing. But there had been no orders to let the old man shoot them down.

Behind him, Will heard his wife coming out of the house. She slipped her arm into his but he stood firm, his rifle pointed squarely at the chest of the man he guessed to be the leader of the four.

'Get off my land!' Will bellowed. 'I'm warning you — this gun ain't for show!'

Zeke Emmett leaned forward in his saddle. 'You gonna shoot all four of us, old man?'

'Just get off my land,' Will repeated but there was anxiety in his voice. He could not kill four men. One maybe, perhaps wing or wound another, but not four. Not before they gunned him and Mary-Anne down where they stood. But he could not stand by and let them destroy everything he had worked for; everything that was part of his life.

Emmett could sense the fear in the old farmer.

'So what do you reckon, mister? Are you gonna use that rifle?'

'What do you want here?' It was Mary-Anne who screamed the question.

Will felt his wife's grip on his arm tighten but he kept his rifle levelled at the man who was clearly the leader of the group.

'Don't worry, Annie. They are not here to kill us. If they were going to leave us dead they wouldn't be hiding their faces. They are just hired guns delivering a message.'

Behind his hood, Zeke Emmett grinned.

'That's smart talk, old man. Now why don't you put down that rifle, collect your lady and move off that porch. Then you will be free to walk away from here.'

Will Horn spat in disgust.

'After we have watched you burn our house to the ground? Like I said, get off my land and tell your bosses it'll take more than four hired hoods to frighten us out of our home.'

Suddenly, the talking ended. The man on the far left of the four night raiders, without warning, unholstered his gun and fired.

The bullet ripped into Will Horn's chest; his wife screamed. Then, another shot . . . this time hitting the woman in the stomach. She screamed again, falling on top of her stricken husband.

The killer fired a third time and removed his hood.

'You talk too much, Zeke. We came here to get these people out of the valley. That's done. Now get on with the rest of the job and set fire to this place. And two of you, get those bodies inside the shack before you put a light to it.'

Zeke Emmett removed his hood. The others did the same and sat in silence as the fourth member headed towards the barn.

Blake Bannon had shown them who was boss of this outfit.

* * *

Vic Bannon turned on his son, anger showing in his vivid features. Dawn was less than an hour away and the lights were dim in the large ranch house that had once been the home of the Lassiter family but now belonged to the Bannons.

'You crazy, gun-happy fool! What did I tell you? No killing. Just scare them off, burn their barn. What was so hard to understand?'

Blake sat in the corner of the room, like a pouting schoolboy, well aware that his father's rage would soon pass; that he would soon see the wisdom of what had happened the previous night. No witnesses.

'The old man threatened us,' said Ray Masson, one of the four night raiders.

Vic Bannon scoffed. 'An old man threatens you so you decide to burn his place to the ground, kill him and his wife and then you come in here and tell me you've done a good job. You're a fool, Ray, just like him,' he pointed mockingly at his son, 'and you too, Zeke. I put you in charge because I thought you had some sense. Oh, I know you like to join in a good whipping, but killing an old couple . . . '

'I tried to — ' Zeke started to say but thought better of it. Sooner or later he would have Blake to deal with and accusing him of losing control would not easily be explained.

Vic stormed across the room and leaned heavily on the arms of the chair in which his son was slouching. He leaned forward and was only inches away from Blake's face when he barked: 'God help us, Blake! Unless these farmers are as dim as you think we could have a range war on our hands — and all because you couldn't keep your gun in its holster. When will you ever learn?'

He sighed, turned away and suddenly seemed drained of all his anger. He knew that his son would never be anything other than a trigger-happy, power-crazed hoodlum. But he was still his son, and that had to count for something.

Throughout the argument, two men

had remained silent: lawyer Frederick Tibbs and Sheriff Luke Franklin.

Tibbs had arrived with all the expertly forged documents needed to force the farmers off the open ranges and claim them for Crawford and Bannon but he would have no part in murder. And, unless he was very much mistaken, Clay Crawford had known nothing of the night's incident.

Maybe it was time to pull out, to give up the idea of becoming mayor of the new Crawford City, though he reckoned if Vic knew about that he would change the name to Bannon Creek. He was still toying with the idea when his thoughts were interrupted by Vic Bannon's voice.

'Now listen good, all of you. Especially you, Tibbs. So far nobody can connect us to what happened last night. Sure, they'll have their suspicions, but that's all they've got. Why would we want to run the Horns or anybody else off their land when we can claim it all legal, like?

'No, this has got to be down to some renegades who have broken out of the reservation. But we are going to need some evidence for Luke here to use against the Indians. So, here's what we do and you, Blake, you take notice of what I'm saying because for once that gun of yours can stay in your belt.'

While Vic outlined his plan, Luke Franklin sat in silence. He had his own ideas on what he could do — and they included making sure that Vic Bannon paid him what was his due or swing at the end of a rope.

6

Jack Crawford had seen death many times — friends and comrades, some younger than himself, butchered, cut to pieces or so full of bullets that their bodies were torn apart like rag dolls. But as he watched the charred remains of Will and Mary-Anne Horn being taken away from the ashes that had once been their home, he felt that he would be violently sick.

The sheriff had been out of town on another of his business trips when Felix Sykes rode in to report what he had seen the previous night.

'Our place is just across the valley from Will's. I couldn't sleep, worrying about Bessie. I went out for a stroll. It was a cold night; the wind was getting up and I suspected we were in for a storm. I was making my way back towards the house when I looked out towards the rise on the east side. I saw a glow in the night sky that could mean only one thing — a fire.

'I couldn't leave Bessie and Jenny was asleep so it was breaking dawn before I hitched up the buggy and headed out there. By the time I reached Will's place there was nothing much left except a burned-out barn and a smouldering house. There was no sign of Will or Annie so I guessed they had come into town to visit Annie's sister. It was a terrible sight, Jack, and I didn't know what to think, except — '

Jack waited for him to go on but when nothing came he prompted: 'Except what, Felix?'

The farmer shook his head, reluctant to carry on. Eventually he said: 'Hell, Jack, I know Clay is your brother but this could be his dirty work. He's been trying to force us small farmers out for more than a year and two days ago he sent that Blake Bannon and his sidekick round to Caleb Jones with a message. It was a message that was delivered with a bullwhip and a kicking. Look, I don't want to be the one to point the finger at Clay but it doesn't look good. Since he teamed up with that Vic Bannon things have got really bad around here.'

That was true enough but now it was no longer a matter of family loyalty. Jack had to talk to his brother. He could not bring himself to believe that Clay had sunk so low that he could be part of anything like a house burning and murder. Had that been exactly what had happened to their parents?

No, Felix had to be wrong. This, this devastation, could have nothing to do with his brother. He refused to believe it.

He was still walking aimlessly through the rubble, kicking over the debris when he spotted it, charred but still visible.

An arrowhead.

Jack studied the small piece of sharpened metal before he started to search through the debris for anything else that could be considered to be evidence. Scorched wood, burned feathers, anything to add to the find he had just made . . . to confirm that this was an Indian raid.

The area had not seen any such attacks since before the war, when groups of renegades from reservations up north went on the rampage. But that was no guarantee that they could not happen again.

He studied the arrowhead. No blood stains, no reason to connect it with the deaths of the two people whose bodies had been found clinging to each other. But how else could it have got there?

He turned to the two men who had accompanied him from town — the clergyman Abel Child and the under-taker Zachary Phipps.

'Right, Reverend, I'll leave this up to you and Mr Phipps to get what's left of these poor folks back into town. There is somebody I have to see.'

He turned and walked sombrely away from the ruins. The Circle-C would not be his first stop. Clay could wait. He wanted to meet his brother's partner Vic Bannon.

★ ★ ★

Luke Franklin had waited for the others to leave the Bannon house. He knew what he had to do was not going to be easy and Vic would be in no mood for a friendly chat.

Planting evidence was nothing new and pinning the blame on reservation runaways seemed the best way to divert attention from the real killers.

'Nobody's gonna dispute it when Luke writes off the attack as an Indian raid,' Bannon had said, outlining his plan for Masson and Blake to return with the arrowhead and charred knife.

Franklin had protested. 'I ain't alone any more, Vic. I've got a deputy. He's Clay Crawford's young brother and he ain't going to believe that this was an Indian raid, even with that arrowhead and other bait.'

'Then it's your job to convince him,

Luke. Remember, if he starts showing signs that he's suspicious you can remind him that we — that's me and his brother — have got no reason to burn the Horns' place. Or any of those other small farms. We've got the papers to show we can make legal claims to the land.'

'But those papers Tibbs has got are forgeries. They've got no legal use.'

Vic had pulled heavily on his cigar and laughed, a raucous, deep-throated guffaw. 'Don't be a fool, Luke. Do you reckon that out here in the wilds of Missouri these people have any notion of their rights? All you've got to do is your job — leave the rest to Tibbs.

'As far as the law is concerned this was a raid by a few runaways down from the reservations in Kansas or up near Jefferson City. I made sure Blake saw to that when I sent him back to put those arrow heads and that knife on the fire.

'Now — what's keeping you here?'

Luke gulped. Now was the time. He

had drummed up the courage to face this moment and there was no going back.

'I want out, Vic. And I want paying for what I've got that's keeping Clay Crawford and his brother out of your hair.'

* * *

Clay stubbed his cigar, finished his whiskey and strode angrily towards the veranda overlooking the grazing land that led to the river. He was angry with himself. The visit to his brother had gone badly. He should never have left things as they were. He recalled what things had been like when they were younger, almost inseparable when they were growing up. It was Clay who had taught his young sibling how to ride, how to rope a steer and, despite their mother's worried protests, how to shoot. Tin cans and bottles at first. Then on to moving targets. Wildlife.

They had worked on the ranch

together, helping their father through a long illness.

He remembered the day that Jack had come home with the news that he was joining the southern army. He had seen it coming for months — ever since the news came through of the riots up in St Louis in May of '61.

The state of Missouri had been sorely divided by the outbreak of the Civil War and when the Union Militia clashed with civilians, causing twenty-eight deaths, including women and children, and injuries to nearly a hundred others, bitterness and hatred grew with a ferocity that got out of control.

Two months earlier the State Constitutional Convention had voted to stay in the Union but when war broke out the vote became meaningless. A pro-Confederate group raided the arsenal at Liberty, Missouri and fears spread among the Unionists that the St Louis arsenal, with its forty thousand or more weapons, would be the next target.

As the unrest grew, governor Claiborne Fox Jackson, a secret supporter of the move to secede from the Union, contacted Confederate President Jefferson Davis asking for heavy artillery to attack the St Louis arsenal and on 9 May a steamer delivered that aid. It consisted of howitzers, thirty-two-pound siege guns and five hundred muskets. The Militia volunteers collected the weapons on the St Louis riverfront and transported them six miles to Camp Jackson.

The following day Union Captain Nathaniel Lyon marched on Camp Jackson with six thousand men to force the surrender of the six hundred Missouri volunteer Militia under the command of General Daniel Frost.

The lengthy march of the prisoners through downtown St Louis sparked the riots that were to become known as the St Louis Massacre.

The report suggested that a drunkard had fired into the crowd of troops, fatally wounding a captain in the Third

Missouri Volunteers. In response the Volunteers fired over the heads, killing twenty-eight civilians.

'Clay, women and children were butchered. We can't just sit around and let them get away with it. I've got to go because . . . because it's the right thing to do.'

Clay remembered how he had gripped his young brother's shirt and dragged him close. He remembered his anger as he spat out the words: 'Family comes first! To hell with the people up in St Louis. We need you. Dad and Mother. And me! You can't go fighting some stupid war that's no concern of ours.'

But the anger had been wasted. Jack had walked away and gone to his war.

Now, almost six years later, he was back and wearing a lawman's badge.

Clay's reflections were interrupted by a noise from inside the house and he turned to see Lucy Dillon. She was carrying two bags and she was dressed ready to leave.

'Where the hell do you think you're going?' It was a question full of anger and that anger was no longer aimed at himself. He had found another target.

'I'm leaving, Clay. I'm going home.'

He stood in the doorway, legs spread and arms folded.

'You'll leave when I say you can leave, Lucy. You just get yourself back upstairs and unpack those bags. You're going nowhere.'

Lucy dropped the bags at her feet. But instead of turning towards the staircase she stood her ground.

'I've had enough, Clay. You've bought out my father, your aunt, the bank, I even heard you are trying to force out the small farmers. You won't be satisfied until you and that Vic Bannon own the whole town, and even then that may not be enough for you.'

Clay grinned and moved towards her.

'When I took you in, I told you what I was planning. You were taken with the idea fine back then. Now, because your old man can't pay his debts on the livery stable you're coming over all hurt and sorry. Well, let me tell you, Lucy. Nobody walks out on Clay Crawford.'

'Well I am walking out.'

Clay stopped in his tracks. He found himself staring at the silver barrel of a derringer.

'Now hold on,' he said hesitantly. 'There's no call for pulling a gun on me, Lucy. I — ' Then, as though a thought had suddenly hit him, he went on: 'This wouldn't have anything to do with my brother turning up sort of unexpected, would it?'

Lucy felt the gun hand tremble.

'Jack's got nothing to do with this. It's you, Clay. You treat me like I was some saloon girl. Well, I've had enough and I'm leaving.'

Clay made a move to intercept her but she regained her nerve and pointed the gun at his chest.

'Don't make me do this, Clay,' she snapped. 'I will if you try to stop me — and there are people in this valley who will thank me if I do.'

Seeing the look in her face, he backed away.

Keeping her gun aimed firmly at him and ignoring the bags she had dropped, she eased her way towards the door and out on to the veranda. Clay stood and watched as she mounted the saddled sorrel tried to the hitching rail. He made one last effort to make her stay.

'You'll regret this, Lucy — you and your father. Like I said nobody walks out on me and lives to shout about it. I'm warning you.'

But even as his voice reached a screaming pitch, she was heading away from the ranch at a full gallop. He went inside the house, headed for the drinks table and poured himself a large whiskey.

'Bitch!' he said aloud before downing the drink in one mouthful. But it was not Lucy Dillon he was thinking about. The name obsessing his entire being was that of Jack Crawford.

★ ★ ★

117

Luke Franklin spent the day killing time along the river and it was late evening when he eventually returned to town from the Bannon house. He was in one of his better moods, having reached an agreement with Vic Bannon over plans to leave Creek Forks at the right price. The old man had readily agreed to pay Luke what he was asking and they had even shared a drink before he left. He wondered whether he had priced his information too low but there was no point in being greedy. Five thousand dollars would suit him fine as a retirement fund.

The town was quiet when he hitched his horse to the rail outside the Aces High and went in. He hoped he might run into Ben Lockhart. He would have taken a lot of pleasure from throwing the silver star at the mayor. Let him see how Jack Crawford liked the idea of being sheriff.

But Lockhart was not in the bar. In fact the only customer was Dan Curtis, one of the names on the list of farmers

Bannon and Clay Crawford were aiming to force out of the valley.

He was leaning on the bar talking in quiet tones to bartender Sam Charnley.

'Over here, Sam,' Franklin shouted, taking a place at his favourite table. 'And give Dan a drink. On me.'

'Not for me, Sam,' Curtis said. 'At least not from him. I'll buy my own drinks while I still can.'

It was said loud enough for the sheriff to hear and he was swiftly up from his seat and across to the bar. He sidled up to the farmer.

'What's eating you, Dan?' he asked. 'Ain't my money good enough?'

Curtis turned to face the newcomer.

'Since you ask, Sheriff,' he answered, glaring into the lawman's face, 'it isn't. I don't want to drink on dirty money.'

Luke Franklin stiffened.

'What the hell you sayin' Curtis?'

'You heard me good enough. I don't want to drink on Crawford money. Or that Vic Bannon.'

Sam slid the whiskey bottle and glass

to Franklin, who snatched it up.

'You ought to be really careful what you're saying,' the sheriff growled. 'Just be grateful I'm in a good mood tonight and am just looking for a quiet drink.'

He turned to go back to his table but Dan Curtis grabbed his shoulder and spun him round.

'That's it, Franklin, turn your back, just like you always do. Will Horn would like to be in a 'good mood' as you call it. But he and his wife are lying in their coffins — what's left of them, that is.'

'Now, look here — '

The sheriff got no further with his attempt to interrupt.

'No, you look. What are you doing about what happened out there? Nothing. You leave it to that young deputy of yours and we know who he is, don't we? Clay Crawford's brother. You turn your back on everything, Franklin and we're sick of it. Well, I'm warning you, if you think you can just wash your hands of what's happening here you're badly mistaken. I'm not the only farmer who thinks you're nothing but a crook. And some of them aren't as obliging as me so I'd be watching my back if I were you. Now, get back over to your table with the only one who can stand your company. Yourself.'

Dan turned away and finished his drink.

'I'd like another, Sam, but there's a smell in here right now, so if you don't mind I'll spend my own money in the White Horse.'

Luke Franklin watched the farmer leave the bar and head towards the saloon across the street. He filled his glass and studied it before taking a drink.

He knew now that it was the right time to get out. If Curtis and the other farmers were of the same mind there would be plenty of blood spilled before there was peace in this valley.

He wanted no part of any range war and the five thousand dollars Vic Bannon had agreed to pay him would be compensation for moving on to California, maybe. San Francisco had always appealed to him. That would be his first choice or maybe further south in Los Angeles. When his wife had walked out on him taking their son with her, she had told him that California was just about far enough away from him.

Well, maybe it wasn't, not now that he was about to become five thousand dollars richer.

The Aces High was gradually filling up when Franklin emptied his whiskey bottle and staggered out into the night. Clouds were rolling in and there was every prospect of overnight rain, but he cared little about what the weather had in store. By this time tomorrow he would be aboard a stage headed north for Kansas City and then aboard a railroad to any city of his choice.

A lone pedestrian grunted a passing 'Good night' as Franklin made his way along the sidewalk. He still had one more act to perform before he finally threw his star into the waste basket and that meant a last visit to his office. Much of the town was in darkness but as he approached the sheriff's office he was surprised to see there was a light on in the room.

Surely young Crawford was not still working at this hour? He would get plenty of opportunity to show that he was indispensable once Ben Lockhart discovered that his sheriff of the past fifteen years was heading out West.

Pushing open the door, Franklin expected to see his young deputy sitting behind his desk, reading the local newspaper or studying one of the law books that had been gathering dust on a shelf these past ten years. Instead he was stunned into a sudden halt in his stride.

The place had been ransacked. Chairs and tables had been overturned, papers were strewn across the floor and even the coffee pot had spilled its contents over one desk. The other had been tipped on its side.

And Sheriff Franklin had a visitor.

'What the hell's happened?' Franklin demanded. 'And what are you doing here?'

The caller leaned casually on the door jamb and grinned.

'Oh, I think you can already see what's happened, Luke. And as for your second question, the answer is simple. This.'

Without another word he pulled his gun from its holster and put two bullets in the chest of the startled sheriff. The visitor hurried out of the office and mounted his horse that he had hidden out of sight around the corner of the building. He was out of town before Luke Franklin had taken his last breath.

7

Jack Crawford knelt over the body on the floor of his office. He got to his feet and tried to take in the wreckage.

He had been awakened by a loud banging on his bedroom door. His deep sleep had been undisturbed since he had retired an hour before midnight the previous night but he was quickly awake and aware of his surroundings.

'Who is it? Who's there?'

'Jack! It's Ben Lockhart.'

The mayor had been like a man close to panic when Jack opened his bedroom door.

'Bad news, Jack,' Lockhart had managed to stammer. 'It's Luke Franklin. He's dead. Murdered in his office.'

The pair had hurried down the silent main street — there were few reasons to rise early in Creek Forks these days — and they were now trying to take in the scene.

'Shot twice in the chest,' Jack said though the cause of death was clear enough. But as he looked at the wreckage, he added: 'Somebody didn't just come here to kill the sheriff. They had other plans. Maybe he walked in on them. Who found him?'

'I did. I was calling on him on council business. The door wasn't locked so I came in and saw him lying there. The lamps were still burning so maybe he had been working late and like you said, somebody came in.'

Jack stepped over the body and started to look around. The place was a mess of spilled coffee, strewn papers, a broken chair and an upturned desk.

'Do you reckon it was a robbery?' Lockhart offered.

Jack smiled. 'What is in a sheriff's office that's worth stealing? Looks to me like somebody had a serious grievance with Luke Franklin. Not only to shoot him, but to smash his office. This seems like the work of an angry man.'

He moved to straighten some of the furniture, including his own desk. As he put it back in its corner position he spotted the broken drawer.

It was the one he had tried to open on his arrival. It had been locked then and he had intended to ask Franklin about that. Now he would never get the chance. The drawer had been prised open and was empty.

Perhaps Mayor Lockhart was not so wide of the mark with his suggestion that robbery had been the reason for the killing of the town sheriff. But what had been taken? What had been so important to be kept in a locked drawer? And had it been the reason that Luke Franklin was now lying dead on his office floor?

'We'll get the doc in to check the body over and then the undertaker can take him away. Did Luke have any family?'

Ben Lockhart thought for a moment, then said: 'A wife, and a young son. Not that he ever spoke of them much. I don't even remember her name. The boy was called Kenny but he and his mother ran out on Luke a few years back. Couldn't stand his drinking. I remember him saying that they were headed for California but after that nothing.'

'I guess the town has enough money to pay for a decent burial, Ben,' Jack said. 'Can you arrange it?'

Lockhart nodded. 'Sure, Jack but, look, I know lawmen have the occasional problem with men they've arrested but I don't think Luke did anything more serious than lock up the odd drunk for the night. Who would want to kill him?'

'That's what I aim to find out,' Jack told him. He was not only thinking about who gunned down the town sheriff, but why? And did it have anything to do with what had been in that locked drawer?

Once the body of Luke Franklin had been taken away Jack spent most of the morning getting the office back to something like normal, cleaning up the spilled coffee, tidying the loose papers and putting a broken chair back together.

He was only two days into his new job as deputy sheriff and already he was faced with the problem of finding a killer among the townsfolk of Creek Forks.

The effort of tidying the office and lifting the furniture had caused Jack's wound to ache and he was settling down on the makeshift bed in one of the cells when he had an unexpected visitor, the Reverend Abel Child.

Jack struggled to his feet and stretched out his hand to greet the clergyman. The thin-faced, almost cadaverous figure tried to break into a smile but it was a tame effort. He was clearly disturbed by the necessity to call on the newly elevated town sheriff.

Jack tried to put him at his ease.

'Hullo, Reverend, what brings you here?' he asked offering his visitor a seat.

Abel Child nodded his thanks, settled in the chair and replied.

'I've just heard about the sheriff, Mr Crawford. Terrible business . . . gunned to death in his own office.'

Jack nodded his agreement but said nothing. It was clear that the man in black was having difficulty explaining the reason for his visit.

Eventually, after a bout of apologetic coughing, he said: 'I am conducting the burials of William Horn and his wife Mary-Anne at noon tomorrow but I suspect that will not be the end of the business.'

'You will have to explain that, Reverend.'

Again the clergyman struggled with his explanation.

'I understand the funerals will be attended by many of their farmer friends from around the county.' When he saw that the lawman was about to interrupt he held up his hands. 'Yes, I know that is to be expected, Mr Crawford, but I fear that will only be the beginning. The Dutchman — I believe Akerman is his name — has asked for the church to be made available for a public meeting after the service.

'He says he wants as many people from Creek Forks and the district to be informed of such a meeting and, well, he has asked me to display this around town.'

He reached inside his long coat pocket, pulled out a sheet of paper and handed it to Jack. The lawman unfolded it and read the message.

WILL HORN WAS OUR FRIEND. DON'T LET HIS DEATH COUNT FOR NOTHING.

CITIZENS AND FARMERS OF CREEK FORKS MUST STAND TOGETHER. MEET AT THE CHURCH AFTER THE FUNERAL.

WE WILL NOT BE DRIVEN OUT.

Jack read through the scrawled message twice before sliding the sheet back across the table to the clergyman.

'What do you make of that, Mr Crawford?'

'Looks to me like the farmers are worried and expecting more trouble.'

'Yes,' Abel Child nodded. 'But from where?'

'We might have to wait to find out about that, Reverend.'

The clergyman shook his head. 'I think we can both guess where any trouble will come from. I'll bid you good day, Mr Crawford.'

The clergyman left but Jack was not alone for long. He was still chewing over what had clearly been a warning from Abel Child when he had another visitor — the barman from the Aces High Bar, Sam Charnley.

'Hullo, Sam. You're a surprise caller. I thought you were chained behind that bar.'

The attempt at a friendly welcome had no effect. Charnley's frown was enough to suggest that he was not paying a social call.

'I ain't sure I'm doin' the right thing here, young Jack, but the sheriff was a sort of friend of mine — least he was a good customer and I don't think he deserved to get what he did.'

'Nobody deserves to get murdered, Sam.'

The barman thought about that.

'Maybe not, but Luke was the law around here. Had been since I got to Creek Forks. Maybe he wasn't everybody's favourite lawman but he didn't deserve to get himself killed. And right here, in his own office.'

That was the third time Jack had heard mention of the killing 'in his own office' as though there was a good place to be murdered.

He waited for Sam to go on but the old man clearly needed a prompt. It had been only four hours since Luke Franklin's body had been discovered and carried away to the funeral parlour. Yet there was Sam Charnley — probably the man who knew the dead sheriff better than most — clearly with something to say.

'Take your time, Sam. If you know something that might help me find out who came here last night and killed our sheriff I'd be happy to hear about it.'

'Well, now I'm here I ain't too sure, young feller. It may mean nothing, just a matter of drink talking.'

'Maybe if you tell me what it is I can decide for myself,' Jack suggested.

'It was last night. Luke came in looking friendlier than I'd seen him in a long time. The place was empty except for one other drinker at the bar. Luke offered to buy him a drink but the other man turned on him. In fact, he called Luke a few names and even threatened him. If Luke had been his normal self I reckon he would have been ready for a fist fight. He had a temper when he was riled — and he got riled pretty easy.'

'So what happened?'

'Like I said, the guy threatened the sheriff and warned him to, well, 'watch his back,' was what he said.

'Thing is, he practically accused Luke and you of being in cahoots with your brother and that Vic Bannon in trying to run the farmers out of the valley.'

Jack thought for a moment. 'And you think that this man might have been waiting for the sheriff to ambush him here in the office?'

Sam shrugged. 'Like I said, it may mean nothing. Just thought you'd like to know.'

'Who was this man, Sam?'

'Not one of my regulars, but I heard Luke say his name. It was Dan Curtis.'

* * *

Little more than a dozen miles outside of Creek Forks, a lone rider dismounted, mopped his brow and walked his horse to the edge of a ridge. Far below, a small shack complete with corral was the only building for as far as the eye could see.

It had been a long journey and both horse and rider were tired and hungry. He had been on the trail for many days and had still to meet anybody who knew of the man he was hunting. Stopovers at small towns had revealed no evidence that the face on the poster in his shirt pocket had passed through but he was convinced that he was on the right track.

It was the face of a killer and this was personal. He patted his horse, remounted and headed down the slope towards the building.

His appearance caused quite a stir in the valley below. Charlie Jackson abandoned the task of fixing the corral gate and ran towards the house.

'Rider coming, Pa!' he yelled. 'Rider coming!'

Joe Jackson emerged from the house and grinned.

'I heard you the first time, son. Go and tell your ma to get the coffee going.'

Charlie hesitated. The Trading Post had not had a single visitor since the stage stopped over during the storm and that was three or four days ago. The next stage was not due in for another four days and strangers were a rare sight these days. He stood rooted to the spot as the rider came ever closer.

'Charlie!' his father yelled a sharp reminder and the boy turned and reluctantly went inside.

Joe Jackson studied the approaching figure. He was sitting tall and straight in the saddle on the back of a huge chestnut but he appeared to be in no hurry to close the gap. He leaned on a post, lit himself a cigar and took time out to wonder what a lone rider was doing heading out this way.

He waited for the stranger to dismount before stretching out his hand in greeting. The man's grip was firm, his unshaven face friendly. The smile reached his eyes.

'Sure pleased to see this place,' he said pleasantly, keeping a hold on his reins. 'We're both just about all in.'

'Then you've come to the right place, mister. I'm Joe Jackson — this is my trading post.' He heard a noise behind him. 'And this here's my son, Charlie. He'll feed and water your horse while you come inside and rest up.'

The man nodded. 'The name's Daley. Bob Daley.'

'Welcome, Mr Daley. Coffee's on and I'm sure my wife can rustle up a steak and eggs.'

'That sounds pretty good to me.'

The two men walked side by side into the house where Sarah Jackson had already anticipated the needs of their latest visitor and was standing at the kitchen stove.

'Are you heading far?' Joe asked when the pair had taken their seats at the table. The man took a long drink of his coffee before answering.

'Not sure,' he said eventually. 'I won't know till I get there. Then I'll know.'

Jackson laughed. 'If that's your way of telling me to keep my nose out of your business, that's fine. Just trying to make conversation. I'll leave you to eat in peace.'

He moved away from the table but the stranger shook his head in apology.

'No, that's not it, Joe. I've been in the saddle for so long I've almost forgotten what it's like to talk to decent folk.'

Jackson slid back into his seat and studied the man. He already had the impression that this was not just an average drifter passing by. Even at the table he had that air of authority about him. His opinion was confirmed almost immediately.

'Fact is, I'm a US marshal trying to find a killer.'

Sarah turned away from her stove and Charlie, who had been standing in the corner admiring the stranger's shining gun and black leather holster, felt his jaw drop. He waited eagerly for more.

The lawman explained: 'About two weeks ago, the bank in Carthage was robbed and the bank teller was killed. There were three of them. One got himself wounded during their escape but got clean away. I've been tracking them ever since.'

He reached inside his shirt pocket and withdrew the crumpled poster he had shown so many times before.

'This is a drawing taken from the description given by a witness who saw the robbery. It may not even be a very good likeness but I keep on hoping.' He unfolded the paper and pushed it towards Jackson.

The trading post owner studied it and passed it back.

'You say this man got himself shot but still got away?'

'That's right. He was hit in the leg. Not enough to slow him down but he would probably need a doc to take a look at it before long. I've been stopping at just about every town between here and Carthage but without any luck so far.'

'You're sure they came this way?'

'Not sure, but it's a guess; that's the best I've got.'

'The only people who have been through here in the last week have been the stage passengers headed for Creek Forks.'

Daley stuffed the paper back in his pocket. 'I don't reckon you're going to tell me that one of them looked like the man in this drawing and walked with a limp?'

Joe chuckled. 'Sorry, can't help you, but Creek Forks is the next town along this trail. Maybe you'll have better luck there.'

'I'm obliged to you, Joe,' Daley said, finishing his meal. 'This is more than my job. It's personal. The bank teller they killed was my brother.'

Daley paid for his meal, the two men shook hands and Joe Jackson stood and watched the marshal remount and ride away. Then, when he turned and went back inside the house, he tried to shake off the worrying thought that he had been less than truthful with the

141

marshal from Carthage.

There had been a man who had passed this way who walked with a limp. It was true, though, that the poster the lawman had been carrying could have been a sketch of just about anybody.

But had Joe Jackson done the right thing? Or had he allowed his friendship with Billy Crawford to cloud his judgement and keep silent about one of the stage passengers? He only had the man's word that he had been confined to a hospital bed for two years and that his limp was the result of a Civil War battle. Was Jack Crawford the bank robber and killer that Marshal Bob Daley was tracking?

*   *   *

Jack Crawford pulled up his horse at the fence surrounding the Curtis ranch and took in the view. He remembered the days when he was just a kid and he and Clay, along with the rest of the

142

boys in the valley families, used to hold their own rodeos: roping steers, riding, racing, and even sometimes shooting. Only bottles and tin cans and later maybe the odd rabbit.

Bobbie Curtis was a member of the group, the steer-riding champion Jack seemed to recall, but he was older than the others and had long since left the territory. Bobbie had never been one of his closest friends but he was as saddened as anybody to learn that the young Curtis had been killed on the opening days of the war, one of fewer than ninety Union casualties in the first Battle of Bull Run. The news had reached Creek Forks only a few days before Jack left to join the Confederate Army.

Nudging his horse forward, Jack felt himself hoping that Sam Charnley's version of the previous night's meeting between Dan Curtis and Luke Franklin was nothing more than an exaggeration of the events. The Dan Curtis he remembered from his days as a youth was a friendly, cheerful neighbour with hardly a bad word to say of anybody.

It was probable that the war, the loss of his only son and the bitterness of the North-South divide could have changed all that — it had changed many people, as he knew from his own experience. Clay was not the brother he had known and loved and was he himself the same man who had left home? His leg wound was a constant reminder of what he had been through for what, in the end, was a losing cause.

Clay had been right about that and almost two years in a hospital bed had been plenty long enough for Jack to think about it.

Now, through no desire of his own, he had been talked into a position of turning against friends and family — and all in the name of the law.

He dismounted and tied his horse to the trunk of a young tree but he had not reached the porch when the door of the house opened.

'That's far enough, young Crawford.'

The voice was sharp, angry. It belonged to the man he had come to see. And Dan Curtis was holding a rifle.

'You won't be needing that, Dan,' Jack said, stretching his arms as a gesture of good will.

'Say your piece and leave,' Curtis snarled. 'But before you do, let me tell you that you can take a message back to your brother. You can tell him that if he and Vic Bannon want this place it will be over my dead body. Now, get back on your horse and tell him that.'

He waved the rifle in an attempt to add strength to what was clearly a warning but Jack stood his ground.

'I'm not here to talk about Clay or Vic Bannon. It's about last night.'

Curtis sneered.

'So, it ain't your brother who's sent you to do his dirty work, it's Luke Franklin, that crooked partner he calls a lawman. What's he been telling you?'

'Look, Dan — '

145

Before he could say anything further Curtis raised the rifle and pointed it at his chest.

'I told you to get out of here, Jack, and that goes for you and your brother. As for Luke Franklin he can go to hell as far as I'm concerned.'

'The sheriff's dead, Dan. That's why I'm here. He was shot last night.'

Curtis's reaction to the news was not what Jack expected. For a moment he was silent, as if stunned by what he had just been told.

'Dead? Franklin's dead?' Curtis muttered as though he had not heard anything beyond that. Then, recovering quickly, he added: 'I can't say I'll be lining up to cry at his funeral but what has it got to do with me?'

Jack studied the man in the doorway. Could it really be that he did not know about the shooting? That it was news to him? Or was he just an accomplished liar and actor?

'You were heard to threaten him last night in the Aces High. Sam Charnley heard your argument.'

Curtis snorted. 'And you think I killed him.'

'Did you, Dan?'

'Well, maybe that's what you Crawfords might want to think but no, I didn't kill your friend, but I'd like to get the chance to put a medal on whoever did.'

'You're not helping yourself, Dan. You marched out of the bar after threatening the sheriff and the next thing we know he's been gunned down in his own office. How do you explain that?'

'I don't. I expect that badge you're wearing means that you're the law around here now. But that doesn't give you the right to come here accusing me of murder. And before you get off my land and stay off it, did Sam also tell you I went in for a quiet drink? And that I wasn't wearing a gun?

'You've got to look somewhere else for your killer but let me tell you this, Jack. Things have changed around here since you and Bobbie and Clay were kids and you will have a long list of candidates. And another thing, if you think that it was renegade Indians who burned out and murdered the Horns then I think you should ask your brother who the real killers are.'

★ ★ ★

US Marshal Bob Daley dismounted outside the sheriff's office, hitched his horse to the rail and mounted the step on to the board walk. If he had expected to see the face of the man he was hunting on a wanted poster he was in for a disappointment. The board on the wall was empty.

He glanced up and down the street, surprised that it was deserted. Even the door of the law office was locked. Puzzled, he crossed the street and headed for the saloon.

Barely two hundred yards away, the small church at the end of the main street of Creek Forks was filled with mourners. Will and Mary-Anne Horn had been popular members of the farming community and their funeral service had attracted almost every able-bodied citizen from the town and the surrounding valley.

The Reverend Abel Child stood in his hastily erected pulpit reading from his Bible. He knew nothing of the people of Creek Forks but now he found himself having to talk about two of its most well-liked citizens, burned to death in a raid on their humble farm. The evidence, he had been told, pointed to a group of Indians on the run from a reservation.

He had since learned that the truth was a long distance from the rumour but he said nothing of that, just as his own truth was a long way from the clergyman now standing before the crowd of mourners. Foolishly, he had not prepared for such days as this.

He looked down on the congregation and almost surprised himself by praying for divine intervention.

It came in the form of the Dutchman Akerman, who suddenly rose from his pew and walked purposefully to the front of the room.

'Hold it, Reverend! Before you start all the preaching and praying there is something I have got to say.'

There is a God, Abel thought, stepping aside. 'Please, sir, come up and say your piece.'

The Dutchman strode purposefully to the front and turned to face the congregation.

'Friends, two nights ago Will Horn was a hard-working farmer and Mary-Anne was a loving housewife. Today they are lying in those two boxes over there ready to be lowered into the ground and we are here praying over their remains. That's not right. They were good people and they harmed nobody.'

Other than a murmur of agreement from a few people, the congregation remained silent and Akerman mopped his brow as he studied the expectant look on the faces in the crowded church.

'Nobody here will say aloud why they are dead. But you — we — all know the reason and we all know that it had nothing to do with Indian runaways.'

Felix Sykes got to his feet.

'But the arrowhead and that burned-out knife that were found in the ashes?' he protested.

The Dutchman scoffed: 'And you call that evidence? Who was it who turned up that evidence? It was our new deputy sheriff, Jack Crawford, brother of the great Clayton Crawford.'

There was a sneer in the Dutchman's voice and he was not going to be put off by what was only a half-hearted protest from his neighbour.

'We all know who's responsible. So who's next? Who's going to be driven out by Crawford, the Bannons and that hired henchman Zeke Emmett?'

Abel Child felt it was time to interrupt but the mention of the name Zeke Emmett forced him to delay. He needed to hear more.

'We have to listen to what this lawyer's got to say,' one of the women in the group suggested. Her husband was the owner of a general store and had already been approached by Clay Crawford. 'Maybe he will come up with an offer we can't refuse.'

'You think so?' Akerman snapped. 'You think that we are going to be offered a fair price for our land, our stock and our crops? Are you crazy? This lawyer has come from Springfield to carry out orders. He had papers to show that he can take our lands and if he doesn't get what he wants, well . . . ' His voice tailed off and his gaze wandered towards the two coffins in the corner of the room. He walked slowly back to his seat among the other farmers and Abel Child found himself struggling to find the words he needed.

Again it was a member of the congregation that saved the anxious clergyman from any loss of face. Dan Curtis did not stride to the front of the congregation. Instead, he rose from his seat and addressed the crowd from where he stood. And there was a mixture of passion and hatred in his voice when he spoke.

'Two days ago I was one of those people who wanted to take the money, move out and leave Crawford and Bannon to it. Not any more — not when you look across the room and see those two coffins over there.

'If we leave now then Crawford and Bannon will have won. There will be no future here for decent people. The Dutchman is right — we've got to stand up to these land-grabbing killers. If we don't do that then the whole future of Creek Forks and the valley will be in the hands of men who care nothing for property, the law or human life.'

He paused before turning to face Abel Child.

'I'm sorry if that offends you, Reverend, but that's how it is.' He sat down.

Child did not know how to respond

so he simply coughed and called for a moment of silent prayer before the short walk to the cemetery.

Eventually, the crowd shuffled out into the hot sun and along the few yards to the burial ground. But Child was not thinking of his duties as a preacher praying over the interment service of two local farmers. He had not come to Creek Forks for that kind of work and his mind was fully occupied with the real reason for his coach journey to the small Missouri town.

He rubbed his leg in an attempt to ease the pain but his mood was vastly improved with the knowledge that he now knew where he could find the man who owed him a whole chunk of money.

Zeke Emmett was within reach.

* * *

The day after the funeral of the Horns, Sheriff Luke Franklin was also laid to rest, a much quieter funeral with only three mourners — Jack Crawford, Mayor Ben Lockhart and Sam Charnley.

A fourth figure sat astride his horse high on the ridge almost half a mile from the cemetery. He had come to witness the last resting place of Luke Franklin. But he was not here to mourn or regret the death of another lawman. He did not raise his hat as the gravediggers lowered the coffin into the ground.

He was not a bereaved family member — he was Luke Franklin's killer.

8

Vic Bannon drew long and hard on his cigar, sipped his whiskey and studied his visitor. He looked younger than his twenty-six years; not tall, not short, clean-shaven with a friendly face and he had entered the house with a slight limp. But from what Bannon could see there was little family resemblance between this man and his brother.

'So what have I done to earn of a visit from the law?' Bannon asked, a strong hint of sneer in his voice. The introductions had been clipped, less than friendly and just as Jack had expected. He had heard enough of the kind of man to expect when he met Vic Bannon and so far he had not been disappointed.

Bannon looked older than he had imagined and his craggy features, close-cropped grey hair and pencil-thin moustache reminded Jack of many of the men he had served alongside during the war.

'This is just a friendly call, Mr Bannon,' Jack said keeping his voice neutral. 'I expect you already know that Luke Franklin was shot dead in his office three nights ago.'

Bannon stubbed his cigar and rose from his chair.

'Sure I know, Deputy. I think I might even say that Luke was a friend. Not close, but a friend.'

'But you didn't go to the burial.' Jack emphasized his surprise but Bannon chose to ignore the sarcasm.

'And you didn't ride out here to tell me that Luke Franklin was dead. So what is it you want?'

'Like I said, it's just a friendly call. I thought it was time to meet my brother's partner. I've already heard a lot about you, but I'm not the sort to believe in stories until I've seen for myself.'

Bannon reached for another cigar

157

and took his time to light it, using that time to study his young visitor. Eventually he said: 'The people of Creek Forks and the Bannons have an agreement. They don't bother me and I don't bother them — that way we stay out of each other's business.'

Jack could have seen that coming. It was a test. Was he going to stand up to Bannon or just walk away?

'Like I said, there are stories.'

When Bannon said nothing, Jack continued: 'There are people in Creek Forks who have told me you take a whole lot of interest in their business. You and my brother.'

The older man's lined face creased into a semblance of a smile.

'And you've asked Clay about this? It would seem to me that would be your place to start — him being your brother and all.'

'Clay's not home to visits from me so I came here. They tell me you've got big plans for the valley and are aiming to buy up all the small-time farmers.'

Bannon blew a cloud of cigar smoke in Jack's direction.

'And is that a crime in these parts?'

'No — that's no crime, Mr Bannon. If that's all you're intending doing.'

'That's all, Deputy. Clay and me . . . well we've kinda come to an agreement that Creek Forks' days as a one-horse town are coming to an end. When the railroad comes through it can be a great cattle town. All we are trying to do is to get the people to see things for what they are.'

He spotted the look of doubt in Jack's face.

'And if you don't believe me then maybe I have a way of persuading you. I'll send my lawyer into town. He's down from Springfield and he's got all the papers I need to buy out the homesteaders. I'm offering them a fair price for their stock and homes but they have no claim to the land. They have no right to put up fences on open range and deny cattle the grazing and water they need. Maybe those papers will convince you that we're doing things all legal like.'

Jack said nothing. Bannon sounded so sure of himself that any challenge now would only add fuel to what was already a fast-developing volatile situation. He replaced his hat and offered his hand.

He knew this would not be the last time he would come face to face with Vic Bannon but the time was not right for a confrontation.

'Ask your lawyer to call in at the office. The quicker I get to see those papers the sooner I'll be able to tell the farmers that you are a law abiding neighbour trying to do the right thing by them.'

The two men shook hands and Bannon followed Jack on to the veranda, watched him ride away and did not go inside until the young sheriff had disappeared from view.

Back in the impressively large living area of the house, his other caller was waiting for him.

'You heard all that?' he inquired, offering the taller man a whiskey.

The other nodded.

'That young man could bring a whole lot of trouble for us unless we do something about him,' Bannon said, looking closely for any reaction from his visitor. 'And by my way of thinking you are the man to keep him under control.'

His visitor emptied his glass in one long gulp.

'You can forget about him, Vic. It may take some time but he'll come round to our way of thinking. I'll see to it.'

'Good. I'm counting on you. Perhaps a little brotherly persuasion might help.'

Clay Crawford slammed his empty glass on the desk.

'I said I'll see to it,' he snapped and walked out of the room.

* * *

Marshal Daley watched from the opposite side of the street as the young rider hitched his horse to the rail and went into the sheriff's office. So far his visit to Creek Forks had turned up nothing in his search for the man whose face was sketched on the sheet of paper in his shirt pocket. Maybe he would have more luck with the local lawman.

But his luck did not change.

Jack studied the drawing before passing it back to his visitor. He shrugged.

'Sorry, Marshal, but that could be just about any man here in Creek Forks. There doesn't seem to be anything to pick him out from the crowd.'

Daley folded the paper and returned it to his shirt pocket.

'I guess so,' he said with an air of resignation. 'I'm told he walks with a limp, if that's any help.'

'Not unless it's supposed to be me,' Jack grinned. 'I walk with a limp. Got it in the war, though, not robbing a bank in Carthage.'

He poured Daley a mug of coffee and

offered him a seat. The visitor accepted, settled down and threw his hat on to the desk.

'Looks like I could be chasing my own tail here, Sheriff. Like I told the man at the trading post, this is personal. My brother was gunned down in the bank raid. And from what I've been hearing since I got into town a couple of hours ago you've got troubles of your own.'

Jack nodded but said nothing. He was interested in hearing what the marshal had been told.

'Runaways from the reservation have been burning houses and killing farmers is what I've heard,' Daley said.

'That's only the talk, Marshal, and maybe not very helpful. It looks to me like somebody is trying to blame the Indians when the real killers could be a lot closer to Creek Forks.'

'Want to tell me more?' Daley said, taking a drink from his coffee mug.

Jack related what had happened at the funeral service for Will and

Mary-Anne Horn, highlighting the outburst by Akerman and the accusations against Vic Bannon.

'I've just been out to Bannon's place. He's not the sort of man you want to tangle with but the accusations against him that he's trying to force out the small farmers and homesteaders by fear could be just that — wild accusations.

'He says he has the papers to show that the settlers have no more rights to the land in the valley than he has and he's lodged claims up in the capital to prove it. He says he is just exercising his legal right by offering the farmers a fair price for their homes — the land is his for the taking.'

Daley rubbed his chin thoughtfully.

'And have you seen these papers?'

Jack shook his head. 'Bannon's sending over his lawyer, a man from Springfield, sometime today. Maybe you'd like to hang around. I may be the sheriff around here but I'm just a few days into the job and I've spent the last two years in an army hospital. Which is my way of saying I don't know the first thing about legal papers and such like.'

With his own search for a killer having reached what appeared to be a dead end, Bob Daley agreed to stay in Creek Forks for a day or two. He already liked what he had seen of the young sheriff and he did not want to see him ground underfoot by a man whose name had crossed his desk in the past.

* * *

Abel Child's new congregation would not have recognized him if they had passed him in the street. Gone were the black clothes of a clergyman and the hangdog look of a man with the worries of the world on his shoulders.

The long, lank hair and the drooping moustache that had been a feature of his appearance on his arrival at Creek Forks were also missing from the man who sat tall and straight in the saddle as he rode through the main street dressed in a crimson shirt and black vest. A six-gun hung at his left hip, the final sign that the change from preacher to gunfighter was complete.

Once he had reached the edge of town without catching the attention of a single passerby, he dug his heels into the horse. An hour later, he pulled the horse to a halt, dismounted and waited for the arrival of the men he had come to meet: Zeke Emmett and Blake Bannon owed him money from the bank raid in Carthage.

Abel lit himself a cheroot, spotted a rock that looked comfortable and settled down to wait. The Carthage raid was to be his last. He had spent several weeks planning it, befriending the bank teller, discovering all there was to know about the transport of wages to and from the bank. It was all about timing; he had learned long ago that there was no point in robbing a bank when the safe was empty.

He had passed on the information to Emmett and Bannon and everything went according to plan. Except the killing. He'd wanted no part of that, but Bannon was a hothead, out of control and destined to end his days at the end of a rope or in a pool of his own blood on some dusty street.

The phoney preacher could not have cared less but it was his family connections that influenced him. He had ridden with old man Bannon and he knew that if he played his cards right, he could earn himself a slice of the good life.

He smiled as he remembered his decision to disguise himself as a preacher. He had convinced the others on the stage journey, especially that young woman to whom, given different circumstances, he would have made his play. But there would be others, many others once he had settled with Emmett.

The new sheriff in Creek Forks was that young soldier who had been on the same stage and as far as Child could see, he was like a little boy lost. His own leg wound, suffered when he was caught by a stray bullet during the getaway, had healed more quickly than he had expected and everything was going according to plan. Now was the time to collect his share of the money.

He checked his pocket watch, the one item he had retained from his clergyman's outfit. They were late and his patience was wearing thin. He threw away the unsmoked remains of his cheroot, got up from his seat on the rock and stretched his thin frame like a man who has just wakened from a long sleep.

He removed his hat and ran his arm across his sweat-soaked brow and gazed into the clear sky. He knew that if they did not come soon he would have to meet them at the ranch — and the old man would not like that.

But such thoughts were dashed in the blink of an eye.

The first bullet hit him full in the back, sending him spinning against a rock. Barely a second later, another bullet ripped into his shoulder and the bank robber-turned-fake reverend crashed to the ground, his hands clutching at his chest as he rolled over in the dust.

High on the hillside, Zeke Emmett grinned. Abel Child had served his purpose and he would be no further trouble. And sharing the money from the Carthage bank between two instead of three had always been the plan. He went back to his horse, rammed the rifle into its sheath and headed back towards the ranch house to report that he had carried out the job he and Blake had agreed.

Creek Forks would have to find another preacher to bury the rest of those troublesome settlers whose time was running out.

★　★　★

Frederick Tibbs was nervous. All the bombast that had brought him so far — to the brink of becoming the mayor of a boom town of tomorrow — had deserted him. Outside the sheriff's office he felt himself to be on the point of making a sudden retreat and heading back to the safety of Springfield. He remembered when Vic Bannon, his former captain in the Confederate Army, had put the plan to him the day they had met quite by accident outside his small Springfield office, he had been more than willing to listen. And what he had heard had filled him with enthusiasm.

They had arranged to meet at the finest restaurant in town — two responsible businessmen discussing some important legal matter over the finest food the French chef of La Rosette had to offer.

That was on the surface, for the benefit of other diners who consisted mainly of Springfield's leading citizens, bankers, tradesmen, people who regarded Frederick Tibbs as a lawyer of some repute. A man of honour.

They did not know the other man

— a stranger in town — but if he was dining at La Rosette's finest table he was clearly a man of some importance.

Under this veneer of respectability was the truth behind this meeting.

'I need a man I can trust, Sergeant' — Bannon sipped at his wine and offered a smile at the reminder that he had been Tibbs's commanding officer — 'so it is fortunate that I happened to meet you this morning. Now I have to ask myself, are you that man?'

Tibbs avoided the tempting opportunity to remind his lunch guest that, had it not been for him, the pair would not be sitting together and enjoying good food and even better wine.

Shooting a Union soldier in the back may not have been the bravest act of the conflict but it had saved Bannon's liberty — and probably his life.

Instead, he said: 'What is it you want, Captain?' — stressing the word captain as a reminder that they were no longer in the army — 'And is it legal?'

Bannon laid his fork down and

pushed his plate to one side. He forced a smile.

'Now, that's for you to decide — you're the lawyer. What I can say is that it will not only make you very rich, but important too. And I know how you like to be important, Mr Tibbs. You will be able to say goodbye to the life of a small-time lawyer in a no-account town like Springfield.'

Tibbs chewed on the final piece of steak from his meal and leaned back in his chair. 'I'm listening.'

'Good. Well, this is how things are. My partner and me — we need some legal work down in Creek Forks, work that might just appeal to an ambitious legal mind like yours.'

Tibbs listened without interruption as his guest explained how he and a man named Clay Crawford had gone into partnership with the idea of building the biggest ranch in the south of Missouri. How a little backwater town would become one of the biggest cattle stations in the territory with the arrival of the railroad.

'We've already joined our two spreads and things are looking good.'

'Then what do you need from me?'

'There are just one or two problems standing in our way. Homesteaders and farmers. We need to get them out as we are going to open up the valley to the cattle drivers from Texas and the south. They're as stubborn as their own mules — they won't listen to reason.'

He thumped the table with his fist so hard that the plates shook and the glasses rattled. 'They just won't listen. We've made them good offers to buy the shacks and barns that are their property.'

'Their homes,' Tibbs suggested quietly. He watched his guest closely. Bannon was trying to keep his anger in check but as he gulped the remains of his wine as though he was finishing off a glass of whiskey, the lawyer could see that he was close to breaking point. He was still waiting for an explanation of what was expected of him.

When it came he almost choked on that final piece of meat.

'Forged land deeds?' he gasped. 'You want me to come down to Creek Forks with phoney deeds to prove that you have the rights to the land around the river?'

Bannon grinned. 'That's about it, Sergeant. Like I said, the neighbours need a bit of convincing. You're a lawyer. Can you do it?'

Tibbs leaned back in his chair and gave the other man the impression that he was thinking over the idea.

Who the hell did this Captain Bannon think he was? Did he seriously think that he only had to shout and his problems would be solved? He may have had a low opinion of the farmers but Tibbs was not so sure. Riding up with a fistful of papers would not convince anybody. But maybe it was worth going along for the ride.

'What's in it for me, Captain?'

'You'll be well rewarded, Sergeant. I can promise you that.'

174

They shook hands across the table. Bannon's promise included the job of mayor of a growing boom town, ten thousand dollars and his own law practice.

What did he have to lose?

'Tonight I'll head back to Creek Forks. You follow on in a couple of weeks.'

Bannon was about to leave when, in an act that suggested it was a matter that had almost slipped his mind, he said: 'There's one more thing. You have to make my partner believe that this is his idea. I'll arrange for you to meet and you can do your legal sweet talking.'

He left the restaurant and Tibbs ordered another bottle of French wine.

* * *

Inside the sheriff's office, Jack Crawford already had a visitor: another lawman.

Frederick Tibbs got the feeling that he was walking into trouble. This was the real test. Even if the papers in his satchel could fool some sodbusters, it was not going to be so easy persuading a sheriff and a US marshal.

Placing the satchel on the desk, he rummaged inside for the fake papers.

'I believe you spoke to my client, Sheriff, and asked to see the documents that entitle him to lay claim to the land west of the river.' Tibbs tried the lawyer smile that had worked with so many clients in the past. But if the new young sheriff was impressed, clearly the older marshal was not.

Jack almost snatched the papers out of the lawyer's hands, then skimmed through them and then passed them over to Daley.

'Looks full of lawyer speak to me, Marshal. What do you think? Let me introduce you, Mr Tibbs. This is US Marshal Bob Daley from Carthage.'

There was a long silence while Daley examined the papers, during which time Jack noticed that Tibbs was becoming more uncomfortable, twice mopping his brow vigorously. It was not so hot in the office.

'It says in here that the territory west of the river is free range,' the marshal said. 'The homesteaders have no claim.'

Tibbs wiped his face a third time.

Jack got to his feet and leaned across his desk, staring angrily into the lawyer's face.

'These people have farmed in this valley from the days before I was born and you're saying they have no rights?'

Tibbs took back his papers. He felt he had got over the worst.

'It's all there, Sheriff. Under the Homestead Act they all had the right to lay claim to a one hundred and sixty-acre piece of land on offer from Washington. But there were certain conditions. After five years the home-steader could file for the deeds by submitting proof of work carried out to the local land office.

'Like it says right there in my report, the local land officer then sent the paperwork on to the General Land

Office in Washington for approval. No such documents ever arrived from Creek Forks.

'Your farmers and their fences are illegal and Mr Bannon and your brother are within their rights to demand the fences be pulled down.'

'And burn houses to the ground and kill people?' Jack snapped.

'I'd be careful what you say about that, Sheriff,' Tibbs replied. 'Throwing wild accusations about isn't a good idea.'

There was smugness rather than a threat in the lawyer's tone. He had won. He had convinced the local law officer that his client was in the right and it had been so much easier than he had anticipated. He made a mental note to rid Creek Forks of this young sheriff as soon as he became mayor.

But visiting US Marshal Bob Daley was not so easily persuaded.

'I think you should leave these papers in the sheriff's care,' the marshal said quietly.

Tibbs had not expected this quick turn of events.

'But why? You have both seen them.'

Daley nodded. 'We have, but the farmers have not. If you want the sheriff to force them to remove their fences and persuade them to sell to your clients, would it not be wise to show them this evidence? After all, Mr Tibbs, you are a lawyer and you believe in evidence. You have just made that clear.'

'Of course,' Tibbs spluttered. He had been taken off guard.

'Good. We will be in a much stronger position if we go along armed with documents from Washington, wouldn't you agree? From what I hear some of these farmers can be pretty mean and they would not take too kindly to having their fences ripped down without official sanction from the law.'

'Well . . . I reckon that will be in everybody's best interests,' Tibbs said eventually. 'But I must warn you, Marshal, Mr Bannon is not a patient man and I am sure the sheriff here will confirm that his brother is of a similar disposition.

'Of course, I will report back to my clients and no doubt you will be hearing from them.'

'No doubt,' Daley agreed. 'In the meantime' — he passed the papers across to Jack — 'your safe is the place for these, Sheriff.'

Tibbs left without another word but once the door had closed behind him, Jack said: 'Thanks for that, Marshal, but there's just one thing — you said 'we'. Are you aiming to stick around? I'm sure I could use your help in persuading the farmers to move on.'

Bob Daley grinned.

'I've nowhere to go now that I've lost track of the man I'm chasing, Sheriff. I've got a few days before I'm due back in Carthage.'

He paused before adding: 'But I won't be staying here to help you to get rid of the farmers.'

'What are you saying?'

'I'm saying it would not surprise me

if those papers you have just stuffed away in your safe are as phoney as the man who just walked out of here.'

* * *

Felix Sykes eased his buckboard to a halt in the late afternoon heat. It would be dark soon and he still had at least an hour's ride ahead of him. He had taken his young passenger into town when he collected the supplies to give her the chance to visit the only ladies' emporium for miles around. Jenny Lang had been a godsend since her arrival in Creek Forks, helping her aunt and uncle with the chores around the house — she thoroughly deserved the new dress and bonnet they were buying for her birthday. The number of times she had talked about that young sheriff Jack Crawford offered more than a hint that, given the opportunity, she would not be slow in attempting to catch his eye.

The volatile situation in the valley may not have been the ideal time to think about social events such as dances and county balls but no doubt such occasions would eventually arise and his young niece should not be left out because she was lacking a pretty dress.

Felix was still enjoying the warm feeling of having helped Jenny to choose her new dress when she suddenly leaned across and gripped his arm.

'Uncle!' Her voice was urgent. 'Look, Uncle!'

He followed the direction indicated by her outstretched arm. Over to his left, among a cluster of bushes, a fully-saddled horse was grazing. There was no sign of the rider.

'Wait here, Jenny,' the old man said climbing down from his seat. He walked slowly across to the horse, took the reins and scoured the area for any sign of a rider. There was none. He had little choice but to hitch the abandoned horse to the wagon and take it back to the farm. He was leading the horse back when he heard it. At first he thought it was simply the sound of a rabbit running through the under-growth. Then it came again, over to his right, behind one of the rocks.

Felix released the reins, allowing the horse to wander off while he went to investigate the source of the sound — and found himself looking down at a bloodstained figure lying in the dust. Felix scrambled over the rock, eased himself down to where the wounded man was sprawled. One glance was enough to tell him that the man was closer to death than life and the noises coming from him were little more than gurgling nonsense.

'Easy, mister, don't try to move.'

It was pointless advice and Felix knew it. This man was in no position to go anywhere. It was only when he removed his hat to form a pillow and his coat to wrap around the wounded man that Felix recognized the stricken figure. The lank hair and the drooping moustache had gone. So, too, had the high-collared coat; this man was wearing a holster and six-gun. He did not need to examine the man any further to recognize the features of the Reverend Abel Child.

But this was no time to look for explanations — this man needed urgent attention if he was to have any hopes of survival.

Without another word, he got to his feet, scrambled back over the rock and hurried to where he had left Jenny waiting in the buckboard.

Gasping for every breath, he explained the grim situation to his niece.

'We have to get him to town, Jenny. He'll die if we just leave him here while we go to collect the doctor. I need your help. Can you do it?'

Jenny took his hand. 'I've seen gunshot wounds before, Uncle. I will do anything I can.'

'Good girl,' he said enthusiastically, gripping her shoulders. 'We've got to move him. He is very weak and will be unable to help us get him aboard the buggy.'

Jenny smiled. 'Let's go, Uncle.'

Together they struggled to carry the injured man across the rough ground and on to the back of the buckboard. Felix did what he could to stem the blood from what he could see were two bullet wounds.

'Sit in the back with him, Jenny. See what you can do to keep him still but we had best be prepared for the worst.'

It was slow progress and the ruts in the road caused the wagon to bounce and rock too often for Felix's liking. He occasionally looked over his shoulder for a reassuring sign from his young niece. But each time her returning look was one of increasing concern.

The streets were in near darkness when Felix arrived in town but he was happy to see a light was shining in the doctor's surgery.

'Stay with him, Jenny. I'll bring the doctor out.'

He hurried up the short staircase to

the surgery, banged on the door and without waiting for an answer pushed his way into the room.

Jonas Carson, the only medical man for thirty miles, was sitting at his desk. One look at the face of his surprise visitor was enough to tell him that there was some sort of emergency needing his attention.

'It's the reverend, Doc, or at least . . . ' Felix quickly realized that this was no time for explanations of something he did not understand. 'It's Abel Child, Doc, he's been shot. And he's in a bad way.'

Doc Carson was on his feet in an instant, bag in hand and heading for the door.

'Where?'

'He's downstairs, in my buckboard. Jenny's with him.'

The pair hurried down the steps, the doctor leading the way but with Felix close on his heels. A quick examination was enough to tell Carson that the man was close to death.

'We have to get him inside, Felix,' he said sombrely, 'but I am not sure there is much I can do to help him. He's lost a lot of blood and — '

The sound that came from the throat of Abel Child was like a death rattle. The man who had been clinging on to life from the moment the two rifle bullets had ripped into his body earlier in the day suddenly gave up the fight. He died in a young girl's arms.

Jenny pulled her uncle's coat over the face of the man she knew as the Reverend Abel Child and climbed down from the back of the wagon.

'We tried, dear,' Felix said trying to offer his niece some comfort. 'We tried.'

'I know, Uncle, but . . . ' she didn't finish what she was about to say.

'Did he say anything?' the doctor asked.

'Nothing that made much sense, just a few words that didn't seem to be connected in any way. I'm sorry. I was more interested in trying to keep him quiet than listening to what he was trying to say.'

'It doesn't matter,' Felix said, 'it is just that I wondered why a man of the cloth would cut his hair, shave and carry a gun and end up dying from two bullet wounds.'

He paused: 'Can you remember anything he said?'

Jenny thought for a moment.

'From what I could understand from his rambling he was talking about somebody called Lawrence, Carthage bank and Quant-something, or something like that. I'm sorry, Uncle, is it important?'

Felix sighed. 'Probably not, dear. What do you think, Doc?'

'I think you ought to see the sheriff, Felix. Unless I'm badly mistaken, the Lawrence he was talking about was not a person. It's a place up in Kansas. And your Quant-something could be William Quantrill, the leader of a band of Confederate rebels who raided the town back in '63. There were stories of pillage, rape, burning and killing civilians, many of them women and children.

'If Abel Child was talking about that then Jack Crawford will want to know why he came here to Creek Forks.'

9

Marshal Daley studied the body that had been laid out on the bench in the back room of Doc Carson's surgery and referred for the third time to the sketch that he had been carrying since the day he began his search for the men who killed his brother in a Carthage bank robbery.

He handed the sketch to Jack.

'It could be the same man,' the young sheriff said. 'There is something of a likeness.'

Daley agreed. 'The witness only had a brief look at the three men so the drawing is only a guide. You know this man as the Reverend Abel Child?'

Jack nodded. 'We arrived in Creek Forks on the same coach. He looked every part the Bible-thumping preacher he claimed to be.'

Daley folded the sheet and stuffed it

back into his pocket. That done, he took a knife from his belt and proceeded to slit the right leg of the dead man's corduroy pants. Ripping the cloth away he revealed a strapping just above the right knee. Beneath that, a healing bullet wound, all the confirmation that Bob Daley needed that the corpse on the table was the man he was hunting.

'All I can say is that Abel Child and Bart Eaton are one and the same.'

'Bart Eaton? Should I know that name?'

'I reckon not, since you've been in a hospital for the past two years and before that were far too busy fighting for your cause. Eaton was wanted in two states that we know about — train robbery and murder in Tennessee and we suspect he rode with Quantrill.'

The mention of Quantrill's name sent a shiver through Jack. Although the pair had fought on the same side during the war, the only thing they had in common was the colour of their grey uniforms.

Stories of Quantrill's exploits as a guerrilla fighter had filtered through to all the battle fronts including Jack's areas of engagement and it was the Lawrence massacre that had cemented Quantrill's notoriety.

It was only a few days after the slaughter of Union sympathizers, including women and children, in the Kansas town that Quantrill's men broke into factions bent on causing chaos and mayhem for the sheer hell of it.

It was one of those breakaway groups that had killed Billy and Martha Crawford, stampeded or butchered the cattle and set fire to the ranch house.

Quantrill himself may not have been directly involved and was long since dead, killed by Unionist soldiers in Kentucky at the age of twenty-seven, but his name still evoked a gutful of hate and anger.

'So, if this is the man you have been

trailing it looks as though your business here is done,' Jack said after a long silence.

The marshal shrugged.

'Maybe not, Sheriff. There were three men in that bank raid and it's pretty clear that they split up after their getaway. If that's the case they must have made some arrangements to meet up again.' He smiled. 'Killers and bank robbers don't normally go their separate ways without sharing out their loot.

'It's my guess that Eaton, disguised as he was like a respectable clergyman, came here to Creek Forks to collect his share of the money.'

Jack nodded. 'And you think that's the reason he was killed?'

'Why else? It means that the others are here in town, or somewhere not so far away. Tell me, Jack, where did Eaton get on the stage?'

'I got on in Fayetteville, Arkansas and he wasn't on board then as I recall. We had three or four stops before we arrived at Jackson's Post. Trouble is,

Marshal, I wasn't paying too much attention to who came and went. He could have got on board at any of those places we stopped.'

'No matter,' Daley said but he was disappointed. He had hit another block although he still had hopes that the trail had not gone completely cold with the killing of Bart Eaton.

He said: 'I'm sure that whoever broke into that bank and killed my brother is somewhere around here, maybe working on one of the ranches or farms. I think I'll stick around and pay a few calls if you don't object.'

Jack Crawford was a long distance from objecting. He was delighted. He had a strong feeling that he was going to need as much help as he could muster if he was going to handle the growing threat of a range war that would rip a whole community apart and bring more bloodshed and killing to the valley.

'Glad to have you around, Marshal.'

'The name's Bob, Sheriff.'

The pair shook hands; Jack already felt he had found a friend he could rely on.

* * *

Frederick Tibbs was trembling, not for the first time that day. The order to leave his fake papers with the sheriff had come as a shock.

Now he was going to have to explain things to Vic Bannon. And, even worse, to Clay Crawford.

The two men were waiting for him when he walked into the Aces High after leaving the sheriff's office. Neither was in the best of spirits and what he was about to report would do nothing to change that.

'Have a drink, Tibbs,' Bannon offered in a hollow attempt to lighten the mood. 'Come in and tell us how we can go ahead and chase those sodbusters with their chickens and pigs off the range. All legal and with the blessing of our sheriff.'

Tibbs took his drink and downed it in one gulp.

'It's not going to be that easy, gentlemen,' he said, plucking up what courage he had left and adding it to that offered by a second whiskey.

'Go on, Tibbs. Explain.'

Was it Tibbs's imagination or was there real menace in those few words from Clay Crawford?

'The new sheriff — your brother, Mr Crawford — has kept the papers. He wants to study them and show them to the farmers.'

Bannon almost spluttered his anger.

'You mean he doesn't believe the papers are genuine?'

Tibbs helped himself to another whiskey. Larger than the first two.

'Not him. There's another lawman with him. A US marshal, name of Bob Daley. He's in from Carthage.'

A lone drinker standing at the end of the bar suddenly turned and studied the trio in the corner. Seth Billings may have been looked down upon by most people in Creek Forks as the town hobo but he knew somebody who would pay well for what he had just heard. He gulped down the last of his beer and hurried out of the saloon.

Bannon and Crawford did not see him leave. They were far more interested in Tibbs's story of his visit to the sheriff's office.

Vic Bannon's quick temper got the better of him and he slammed his fist down on the table.

'You got to knock some sense into that brother of yours, Clay,' he snapped. 'If we don't get him to hand back those papers and this marshal checks them out at the land office in Springfield — '

'He'll find nothing,' Tibbs interrupted. 'I paid good money for those deeds.'

'Shut up, Tibbs. You've had your chance. Now we'll do it our way.'

'But, you can't — '

Frederick Tibbs's protest got no further. Vic Bannon reached forward, grabbed the lawyer by his lapels and dragged him across the table.

'I told you to shut up! We've got enough trouble without having a US marshal breathing all over us because you loused up. Now, I suggest you get out of here and let us sort out your mess.'

He pushed Tibbs violently in the chest and he was sent crashing over his chair and on to the saloon floor. Scrambling hurriedly to his feet, the frightened lawyer rushed out into the street. It was time to get out of town and go back to take up his old position in Springfield. This easy-money job that Bannon had promised him when they met in La Rosette restaurant was turning into a nightmare that included arson and murder.

Frederick Tibbs would abandon his hopes of becoming mayor of any Crawford City, collect his belongings from his hotel room and head for the stage depot to book his seat on the next coach out of town.

Zeke Emmett threw two dollar bills into the dust and grinned as Seth Billings scrambled to pick them up. The old man knew all about Emmett's lawless past but he was more than happy to carry out the ranch-hand's orders to keep his eyes and ears open for strangers in town.

'Especially lawmen,' Emmett had insisted.

And bounty hunters, Billings had thought at the time but kept the notion to himself. The pay was not good, only enough to keep him in beer and the occasional cheap whiskey at the saloon.

'That's half the pay for half a job, old man. I want to know what that marshal's doing in town. Now get on that horse and get back into town and keep your eyes and ears open.'

Seth stuffed the dollar bills into his hip pocket, touched his battered hat as a sign of mock reverence and climbed laboriously into the saddle.

'I'll be back soon as I hear anything, Mr Emmett,' he said, heading away from the ranch.

Zeke watched him go before settling down to enjoy a smoke.

Marshal Bob Daley from Carthage. He knew that could only mean trouble.

It was only four weeks since they had emptied the town's bank and that crazy teller had tried to be a hero. The three had split up after the robbery and had agreed to meet up again here at the ranch. When, after three weeks, Eaton had not put in a show, the two of them had decided that a half-share was a lot better than a three-way split.

He had been surprised and amused to see Eaton turn up in a preacher's garb to arrange a meeting for the share-out. But that had been taken care of. He had turned the Reverend Abel Child — alias Bart Eaton — into food for the buzzards.

He flicked the remnants of his cigar into the dirt, and strolled across to where he had left his horse.

It was time to make plans for the future of Marshal Bob Daley. And that meant he had to make a call to the big house to have a serious talk with his other partner at the bank robbery. He did not expect Blake Bannon to be pleased.

★ ★ ★

Jack got up to greet his visitor but there was no welcoming smile to go with the handshake.

'Clay, what brings you here? Second time in three days — must be something important.'

The older of the Crawford brothers dragged a chair across the floor and settled across the desk from the lawman.

'We've got to talk, Jack, and you are right, it is important.'

Jack rested his elbows on the desk and smiled.

'Let me guess. It's about the settlers out on the range.'

Clay rose from his chair, putting him in a position he felt was his own, looking down on his brother.

'There's things you've got to get straight, Jack. A lot has changed since you went away. When our folks got killed in that raid back in '63 I was left to struggle on. It damn near killed me but I owed it to them to get the ranch back up and running.

'Sure, I got a lot of help, especially from the Lassiters. But then they sold their spread to Vic Bannon — '

'And he became your partner,' Jack interrupted.

'Vic reckoned he had had his eyes on a place in this part of Missouri so he took the chance to buy the Lassiter spread. From that day, things picked up at the Circle-C and we decided to link up to make one big ranch.'

'But you reckoned without the farmers whose property stands between the Circle-C and the Lazy-L along the river.'

'It isn't their land, Jack. They never

signed any deeds or laid any claims. It's open range and Vic Bannon sent you the papers to prove it. Tibbs, the lawyer from Springfield, brought them for you to see.'

'And I'm having them checked out, Clay. Just to make sure that they are what you and Vic Bannon claim them to be.'

Clay had tried to keep his temper under control during the conversation but he eventually snapped. Slamming his fist down on the desk, he barked:

'What the hell's wrong with you, Jack? There's a railroad coming through here and that means money. Big money. Don't you think Ma and Pa would want that for us . . . for both of us? Vic has made all those farmers and homesteaders a good offer for their shacks — most of them are rundown or falling down anyway.'

'Or like the Horns' place, burned down.'

'That was Indians!' Clay snapped. 'Runaways from up state!'

It was Jack's turn to lose his temper.

'There are folks around here who don't believe that, Clay — and I'm not sure that you do. The arrowhead and burned knife we found could just as easily have been thrown in there to put us off the trail. Tom Horn and his wife were gunned down. Just what would Vic Bannon do to get his hands on that land? His son's already given Caleb Jones a good beating and threatened him with worse.'

For a brief moment, Jack sensed that he saw a flicker of concern cross his brother's face but the impression came and went in a flash.

'Are you suggesting I'd be mixed up in something like that, brother? And why would Vic want to do that when he's got the law on his side? All he has to do is agree a price with those people — '

'Those people! Is that how you see them? They were our neighbours and friends.'

Again the elder Crawford snapped

back: 'That was a long time ago, Jack. We ain't kids any more and this isn't the Creek Forks you left behind.' There was deep bitterness in his voice when he added: 'And I'm not the big brother you ran out on to fight that stupid war.'

Jack sighed. There did not seem much more to say. The man in his office was not a brother. He was a stranger. They may have carried the same name, had the same parents but as far as both of them were concerned that's where it started and finished.

'If you'll excuse me, Clay,' Jack said quietly, 'I've got a council meeting to attend. I'm being officially sworn in as the new sheriff of Creek Forks.'

Clay was about to storm out of the office but he stopped, his hand on the door knob. He turned.

'I'm sorry it's turned out like this, brother. But you can't say you haven't been warned. If trouble comes because of those farmers it will rest at your door.'

Jack watched his brother leave and

through the window he saw him cross the street and head into the Aces High Casino.

10

Mayor Ben Lockhart banged his wooden mallet on the table and made another call for order. The meeting of the local council was in disarray. All had been going according to the planned agenda of house building, road clearing and sanitation problems when the door burst open and the group of farmers marched into the room.

Caleb Jones and the Dutchman Lars Akerman stood shoulder to shoulder at the head of the crowd. Without hesitating, they marched the length of the room and turned to face the large gathering in attendance at the council meeting, which Ben Lockhart had thrown open to the public.

Standing at the back of the room, Jack Crawford, newly sworn in sheriff of Creek Forks, waited for order to be restored. He turned and was surprised to see that Felix Sykes and his pretty young niece were among the group that Caleb had led into the meeting.

The Dutchman raised his arms and the crowd quickly fell silent. 'Sorry to break up this little gathering of the townsfolk, Mayor, but we'd like to ask our new sheriff a question.'

The mayor moved in to protest.

'You cannot just force your way in here and start shouting your orders.'

Jack pushed himself away from the wall.

'It's fine, Mayor. Let's hear what they have to say.'

'We want to know what you are going to do about jailing those who killed Will and Mary-Anne Horn.'

'And putting that crazy Blake Bannon behind bars!' Caleb shouted. 'You all saw what he did to me because I won't touch his old man's dirty money.'

'And Clay Crawford's in it with them!' somebody shouted from the crowd.

Heads turned towards Jack as he walked up the aisle between the rows of chairs. He could feel the hostility towards him but this was not the time to show any signs of weakness.

'Caleb.' He nodded towards the man who had been among his father's best friends. The cuts and bruises were healing slowly but the marks of the beating were still visible. 'Are you planning to make a complaint against Blake Bannon? It'll be your word against his and that won't be enough to keep him in jail for too long.

'As for the killings of Will and Mary-Anne Horn, where's the proof?'

'Well, we sure as hell know it wasn't Indians. There's been no runaways from the reservations reported these last six months. It was Bannon and his gang. And your brother is one of them.'

There were shouts of agreement from the crowd.

'Now, hold on, Caleb, you've got no cause to start accusing people who are not here to defend themselves.'

It was the mayor who sprang to Jack's side.

'It's all right, Ben. Caleb's angry and rightly so but let me tell you all,' he said turning to face the crowd 'Clay's just left my office and he knows nothing about the killings.'

'Pah! You expect us to believe that?' Akerman shouted. 'They want us off our land and they will do anything to make us leave.' He paused but only to gather his breath. 'Well, here's a message to take back to your brother and his murdering friends. We are going nowhere. This is our land and if they think they can pick us off one by one they are in for a shock. We are not leaving.'

There were loud cheers of agreement from everywhere in the hall. Most of the people had lived in the town and the area all of their lives and had happily traded with the farmers and homesteaders since before the war.

'There'll be killing, Sheriff,' the Dutchman continued, 'and some of us will die. But as sure as God is our judge we will not die alone.'

He elbowed his way past Jack and headed out of the hall. In a desperate attempt to calm the situation, the young sheriff grabbed Caleb Jones's arm as he tried to follow.

'Caleb, you've got to stop this. You are farmers, not gun-fighters. You'll be torn to pieces. If Vic Bannon and' — he paused — 'and Clay are behind these killings you have got to let the law handle it.'

Caleb looked into Jack's face. The farmer's eyes were cold, almost unseeing.

'You always were a good boy, Jack. But Clay's your brother and this is no Cain and Abel Bible story. As Dutch said, we may all get killed but at least we will be buried in our own ground.'

He shrugged himself free and marched purposefully away. The rest of the ranchers followed him out into the street.

Only one person stayed behind to offer support for Jack, but Jenny Lang was not sure if she would be able to help. And when he walked right past without a second glance she knew that now was not the time to put that to the test.

* * *

'Are you not hungry, Jack? It's not like you to leave food on a plate 'specially when it's your favourite pie.'

Alice Bailey looked across the dining table at her young nephew who was deep in thought. He had said nothing during the meal and had done little more than push his food around the plate.

'Sorry, Alice,' he said eventually, 'I've got a lot on my mind and I'm not sure I am the man to handle it.'

Alice slid on to the chair opposite. 'Would it help you to talk about it?'

Jack sipped at his coffee and stared into space for a long time before answering.

'There's trouble in the air, Alice. Big trouble. You know better than most what's been happening around here ever since the war ended. Seems to me like most of the town is owned by this Vic Bannon.'

'Including the bank and my store,' Alice interrupted as a sharp reminder.

Jack nodded. 'The livery stable, general store and the Flag Hotel. Now Clay and Bannon have the farmers and the homesteaders running scared. They have brought in this lawyer from Springfield showing deeds that Bannon's Lazy-L and Clay have laid claims to the areas of the valley occupied by the other farms.'

He toyed with his coffee cup, accepted a re-fill from his aunt and then added: 'If those papers are real then the families who have been farming that land for years will have to move out.'

'And the Bannons and Clay will own even more of the territory.' His aunt finished the observation. 'I see why you are worried, Jack.'

'But that's not the end of it,' he replied. 'I've still no idea who killed Luke Franklin or why they ransacked the office. I don't even know if they took anything because I hadn't had the opportunity to check things out, except . . . ' his voice tailed off when he remembered how the locked drawer had been smashed open and was lying on the office floor.

'Except what?' Alice asked, curious, but Jack was on his feet in an instant.

'Sorry, Alice — got to get back to the office.'

* * *

Bob Daley liked what he had seen of young Crawford. The kid would make a good lawman but he might need a little help along the way.

Daley had been a US marshal for more years than he cared to remember but he could still recall the days when he had needed a push in the right

214

direction. It was now time for him to give Jack Crawford that push.

He was sitting at his hotel room window, looking along the main street when he spotted Frederick Tibbs leaving the saloon. He appeared to be in a hurry and more than a mite flustered. Hurrying across the street, Tibbs disappeared under the overhang of the sidewalk below Daley's window. He was heading back to his room, which Daley knew was only three doors along the landing from his own. He waited for the sound of footsteps along the corridor, and then heard a door open and close with a slam.

He grinned privately. Mr Tibbs was clearly not in a very good mood — with somebody. There would not be a better time to confront the Springfield lawyer.

He made his way quietly along the corridor, peered over the balustrade to check that the desk clerk was too busy to take any heed of what might be happening over his head, and tapped gently on the door of room number four.

'Who is it?'

'Message for Mr Tibbs,' Daley said in a voice he hoped sounded something like a messenger.

The door opened and, without waiting for his invitation, Daley pushed his way past the rotund figure and into the room. Already there was an open bag on the bed half filled with clothing.

'Going some place, Mr Tibbs?' Daley said, closing the door behind him and leaning against it.

'What do you want, Marshal?'

'Well, there are one or two things I'd like to know before you leave town.'

The lawyer looked nervously at his unexpected visitor. He was in a hurry to leave and he could have done without a call from a US marshal.

'Then please make it quick; I have a stage to catch.'

Bob Daley moved towards the other man, who edged away, falling back on to the bed.

'Then let's start with those papers you brought with you from Springfield.'

'What about them?'

'Well, you know and I know that those papers are false — that if I go to Springfield, Jefferson City, or any other land office between Washington and El Paso, Texas, there will be no record of any land claim by Vic Bannon. And any claims on behalf of the homesteaders will have been destroyed. By you.'

Tibbs got to his feet and set about finishing the job of filling his suitcase.

'I don't have to listen to this,' he snapped, 'like I said, I've a stage to catch.'

Daley pushed him in the chest forcing him further back on to the bed.

'I reckon you are going to miss your stage, Mr Tibbs, because right now I have more important things for you to do.'

Tibbs recognized the words as a threat and he could only guess what was coming. He had never been a brave man and the thought of physical violence was enough to open his mouth. After all, he was heading out of Creek Forks and had given up on the idea of ever becoming the town's mayor.

Within ten minutes, Marshal Bob Daley had all the answers he needed. It was time to get back to the sheriff's office. And it would help his cause to drag the crooked lawyer with him.

When the pair arrived at the jailhouse, Jack, back from his uneaten lunch, was busy searching through the drawers and cabinets.

'Got a present for you, Jack,' Daley announced, pushing Tibbs into the room. 'Our friend here has something he wants to say.'

By the time Tibbs had finished, the young sheriff had the whole story of how Vic Bannon had secretly — over a lunch in Springfield — arranged for the lawyer to meet Clay and produce what Crawford would believe were papers proving that the homesteaders had no claim to the land. Using his powers of persuasion as a lawyer Tibbs had convinced Clay Crawford that he was doing nothing illegal.

'The fool fell for it.' Tibbs finished by way of a parting shot. 'Vic Bannon's the brains behind it all. Your brother is just a willing stooge.'

11

Lars Akerman finished the wood chopping and threw the axe into the pile of logs at the side of his barn. He had been toiling hard all morning in an attempt to work off the anger that had grown with intensity since the moment he stormed out of the town council meeting the previous day.

He had nothing against the young sheriff but he could hardly expect the kid to arrest his own brother on the say-so of a bunch of homesteaders and small farmers. On the journey home, he sensed that Caleb for one had been wavering in his determination to fight should things take a turn for the worse.

'It would mean a range war, Lars,' Caleb had argued. 'And we are not gunfighters.'

'Does that mean because we are not gunfighters we are cowards? That we have to just take what Bannon and Crawford and his bunch of hired killers throw at us and walk away? Is that what you are saying, my friend?'

Others had joined in the argument and Akerman had a growing feeling that he would be standing alone against Bannon and his men. If that was to be the case then it was time to take action of his own.

Without his small farm there was nothing.

Ever since the death of his wife Elsa, another innocent in the bloodshed of the closing skirmishes of the Civil War, his life had been that of a lonely man. It was true his neighbours had tried to offer their support and comfort and for that he had been grateful, but the days were hard and the nights were long.

Maybe the time had come to do for himself and his friends what the law would not do for them: rid the valley of the Bannons and Crawford.

It could be that they would get to him first but at least if he died he would not be killed as a craven coward like the others. They had seen Will and Mary-Anne Horn killed and done nothing about it. They would rather believe that it was the work of renegade Indians on the run from some Kansas reservation.

He was still thinking about how he would carry out his one-man vengeance mission when his two callers arrived. As they approached, he recognized young Crawford but the other man — taller and straighter in the saddle — was a stranger.

Akerman waited for the two men to dismount before striding forward to meet them.

'What brings you all the way out here, Sheriff? I hope it is not a social call. I don't have the time or inclination to entertain members of the Crawford family.'

'No, Mr Akerman, this isn't a social call but you might like to hear what I have to say. This is Bob Daley, a US Marshal from Carthage.'

The Dutchman nodded a silent acknowledgement of the stranger.

'Then get it over quick, Sheriff. I'm a busy man.'

Daley nudged Jack aside. 'That doesn't sound too friendly, mister. Not when we have come out here to give you good news.'

Akerman showed no signs that he was impressed by the presence of a US marshal at Jack Crawford's side. Instead, he remained silent.

Jack stepped in. 'We've come to tell you that we are on the way to the Circle-C and then the Lazy-L to tell my brother and Vic Bannon that their big-time lawyer from Springfield is keeping a cell warm in the Creek Forks jail. The papers he had were fakes. They have no claim on any of your land.'

The Dutchman let out a sneer of contempt.

'We already knew that, Sheriff. It didn't help the Horns and it won't stop Bannon or your brother from trying to run us out. But as you are going their way, you can give them a message from me and the rest. We are ready for them.'

'Don't be a fool. The law's on your side now.'

Another sneering reply: 'Like I said, the law didn't help the Horns. Now, if you'll excuse me, I've got work to do.'

He retrieved his axe and walked back to where he had been chopping logs.

The two lawmen remounted and Daley observed: 'He's a bit of a hothead, Jack. You could still have trouble with him.'

'Then I reckon we should call on the others before we visit the Circle-C and my brother.'

* * *

They were given similar receptions at the homes of Dan Curtis, Caleb Jones and Frank Miller and it was only when they reached the small farm of Felix Sykes that they were made welcome.

But even when Jack told them that the papers Tibbs had been brandishing were fake, their greeting was tempered by the news that Felix had already decided to leave the valley.

'My wife is not at all well and this conflict with Bannon and your brother is not helping. So now that Jenny is settling into her position at the school and has spoken to Alice Bailey about taking a room at her guest house, we have all agreed that it would be best for everybody if we accept the offer.'

Felix looked anything but happy with the idea of selling up and moving out but Jack understood that his concern for a sickly wife overruled his own preference.

'I'll be sorry to see you go, Felix. I hope my brother has made you a good offer. This is good land for cattle.'

The old man looked tired, almost as if the fight had gone out of him.

'Not what we would have wished for, Jack, but enough to get Bessie and me off to Colorado, maybe even California.'

'How much, Felix?' Jack pressed.

'Same as he's offered all the others,' Felix said dolefully. 'Two thousand dollars. Bannon's sending a man round tomorrow with the agreement. He says he's only buying the house — the land is his for the taking because we've got nothing to prove we own it under the Homestead Act of '62.'

Jack turned to Daley. Then back to Felix.

'When Bannon's man comes round tomorrow tell him the price has gone up, Felix. Tell him you want ten thousand dollars.'

Felix rubbed his chin.

'I don't know, Jack. I've seen what they did to Caleb. And what about the Horns? I'm not fit enough to fight them, Jack. And there's my wife and niece to think about.'

Jack tried again to persuade the farmer to delay the sale but when the lawmen left the Sykes house he knew that any pressure from Bannon would be enough to persuade Felix to take the offer.

Darkness was closing in when the duo reached the town limits of Creek Forks. It was too late to call on Bannon or his brother. They would have to leave the showdown until the following day.

'Let me buy you a drink, Bob,' Jack suggested as they rode slowly towards the Aces High Casino. 'A beer in Bannon's bar will show that we are model citizens and we don't take sides. We even patronize a man who doesn't need our money.'

'And we might learn something that will come in useful,' said the US marshal with a wide grin. 'I accept your offer, young feller.'

★　★　★

Darkness was welcome to Blake Bannon and Zeke Emmett. Secrecy was important and they would have been crazy to hold their meeting at the ranch so they sat across the glow of a dying camp-fire.

Bannon felt his anger growing.

'The marshal knows nothing, Zeke. You got rid of Bart Eaton so the law can't tie us in to the Carthage bank robbery.'

Emmett was not convinced.

'A lawman who rides all this way won't give up easily and he won't go until he's found the men he's looking for. And that means both of us, Blake. Not only me.'

Blake Bannon poked a stick aimlessly into the fading embers of the fire. He was getting tired of Zeke Emmett and his constant complaining. The one man who could have betrayed them was now buzzard bait so the only link to himself and the Carthage bank robbery was Zeke.

Maybe it was time to cut that link. Zeke knew too much, and not only about the bank robbery. Killing Zeke would solve a lot of problems both for himself and the old man.

He was still mulling over the idea of putting a bullet in Emmett and rolling his body down the nearest ravine when the decision was taken out of his hands.

'You're a fool, Blake,' Emmett said quietly. 'Just like you were a fool when you thought that killing that drunk Franklin would get you and your pa out of a hole.'

Blake stiffened. He thought he had covered his tracks well after the shooting of Sheriff Luke Franklin.

'You even smashed up the place to make it look like a robbery. But what's to steal in a sheriff's office? A set of cell keys? Two, maybe three rifles? A coffee pot?' Emmett sniggered at the thought. 'You already know how to make rotten coffee, Blake.'

Bannon looked closely at the man on the opposite side of the fading fire. He had never really liked Zeke and had suffered his company as a matter of convenience. How he knew who had killed Franklin was a mystery, unless he had been there. On the sidewalk outside the sheriff's office. A witness to the shooting.

'But don't worry, Blake, old friend,'

Emmett said, breaking into his thoughts. 'Your secrets are safe with me. So' — another snigger — 'if you're thinking you can solve your problems by putting a bullet in me here while nobody's watching, don't do it. You see, I convinced our late friend, Franklin that those wanted posters he kept locked away — the ones you were looking for when you smashed up his office — would be a lot more valuable if I kept them in a safe place.

'I can say they cost me a lot more than I wanted to pay but, well, let's say I got my money back by cutting Eaton out of our bank share.'

Blake got to his feet and stood over the other man.

'You'll pay for this, Zeke, I swear to God — '

'Hey, now hold on, Blake. Don't you go calling on God for help because he sure won't be listening to you. We've got a half-share of those forty thousand dollars we stacked away; maybe it's time to move on and leave your old man to his beef and his private fight with the sodbusters.'

Blake shrugged. Zeke Emmett was a fool if he thought that he would ever leave the Lazy-L with twenty thousand dollars in his saddle-bags.

'Quarrelling ain't going to do us any good, Zeke. Let's get over to the Circle-C and give Crawford a call. It won't be long before he needs all the friends he can get. Maybe he ain't gonna be around too much longer.'

Zeke nodded but said nothing. He knew the day would come — and come soon — when it would be Blake or him, but not both, who would walk away from a heated argument. Until that day came he would be sure he did not turn his back on young Bannon again.

★　★　★

Vic Bannon was angry. He drew heavily on his favourite cigar, marched across the room and glared at his son, who had arrived home well after midnight.

'You're a damn fool, Blake. Have you

not learned anything since we got here?'

His son shrugged, said nothing.

Vic stubbed out his smoke and quickly lit another.

Maybe he had got it wrong. Maybe buying the Lassiter spread had not been such a good idea after all. At least not for Blake.

He was like any other motherless kid: restless and eager for a life on the wild side. Ranching was not for him.

Vic could hardly blame his son for that. He could remember the days when he would have felt exactly the same. But he had set his sights on the Lazy-L from the moment he arrived there more than four years ago.

Things were different then. The war was on and Vic Bannon and his fellow Confederate rebels were on the run.

It was only a few days after the Lawrence massacre when the off-shoot of Quantrill's forces arrived at the Lazy-L.

Bannon had felt nothing for the Union-lovers in the Kansas town who had been surprised in their homes of the night of 21 August 1863. More than a hundred and fifty of them had died but Captain Victor Bannon preferred to think of the forty men in grey uniforms who had lost their lives.

Somebody had to pay for that and the Lassiters, with their sympathies in the South, had offered a safe haven while he and the six men who had fled with him fed and rested for the night.

'Listen, Blake,' the old man said, sliding on to the arm of his son's chair and softening his voice as a sign of fatherly affection. 'Zeke Emmett isn't a problem we can't handle when the time comes. He's got something I need and so long as we keep him sweet — '

'And away from Crawford,' Blake reminded him. 'What's to say he won't sell you out when he gets the chance?'

'I agree there's a chance of that, son, but he'll be cutting his own throat.'

Vic Bannon refilled his whiskey glass. 'Reckon I'll turn in, Pa, but I warn you to keep an eye on Zeke. I know he can't be trusted.'

He left the room and Vic strolled out on to the veranda. It was a clear, cloudless night offering enough light from a full moon and a myriad of stars for him to stand and admire the distant slopes and the silent herds.

Alone, he considered the future.

This was not going to plan. Buying the Lazy-L was just the start. From the moment he had first set eyes on the valley Vic Bannon had his sights on building a cattleman's empire. Buying off the farmers and homesteaders was going to be easy. Failing that he had the men and the means to frighten them out of the valley. But now Frederick Tibbs and his papers had been exposed as fraudulent and the arrival of the US marshal, who was now closer than he knew to finding the three men who robbed the bank in Carthage, could force Bannon into action.

First, though, he had to make sure that the marshal went back to Carthage empty-handed, and chasing shadows.

It was time Blake went on a trip.

Bannon went back inside the house to make the plans for his son's temporary disappearance.

★ ★ ★

The late night lamps were burning in the sheriff's office. While the rest of the town of Creek Forks slept, two lawmen, Jack and his new friend Marshal Bob Daley, were sharing a drink.

They had been discussing the mounting tension between the farmers and the two big ranch owners but for a change the discussion was not about the threat of a range war between the two factions. Jack got up to stretch his legs.

'What is it that got Luke Franklin killed?' he asked, not for the first time. 'And did the killer find what he was looking for?'

'The drawer was locked for a reason,' Daley said. 'I know when I was local sheriff I used to keep papers, documents and certain wanted posters under lock and key. There are certain things you don't want to be found.'

Jack poured them another drink.

'Tell me about it, Bob.'

The marshal placed his whiskey glass on the desk.

'A sheriff — any sheriff, including you, Jack — needs to know who his friends are. And he has to keep his secrets.'

'Go on.'

'When I was the lawman up in Nebraska I found that the more I knew about the mayor, the councillors and the local businesses and landowners the better. Luke Franklin would be no different. Whatever he was keeping in that drawer was a secret that got him killed.'

'Why would a sheriff want to keep any Wanted poster under a lock and key?'

Bob Daley grinned.

'Not every lawman is as honest as

you, Jack. I've known a few who would hide posters away and use them only when the time came. Half the sheriffs I've run into are nothing more than bounty hunters. Guns for hire.'

Jack thought about that. Was Luke Franklin just a hired gun? Had he kept wanted posters and other crucial documents locked away in his drawer to use later to his own ends? If that was the case, whoever had killed him must have known that.

'So you think Franklin may have been killed by a bounty hunter?' he asked tentatively.

Again Daley grinned. 'Or more likely by somebody whose face and name was on one of those posters. And whoever it was knew what he was looking for.'

Jack slumped back into his chair.

'Seems to me, Bob, I might never find who killed Luke Franklin.'

'Don't give up so easily. From what you have been telling me there is one man around these parts who might know exactly what is going on and what sort of man Luke Franklin was.'

He waited for a response but when none came, he added: 'I think we should be paying a visit to that man, Jack. I'm talking about your brother.'

Jack thought about that, then nodded.

'You may be right, Bob. I think we should call on him early tomorrow.'

★ ★ ★

They found Clay Crawford lying face down on the kitchen floor, his legs twisted awkwardly under him.

'Wait there, Jack,' Daley said quietly, moving forward to examine the body on the floor. Rolling him over, the US marshal looked for any tell-tale wounds.

'Is he dead?' Jack asked, his voice little more than a whisper.

Daley got to his feet.

'Drunk!' he answered angrily, picking up the empty whiskey bottle that had rolled under a table. Another, only half empty, stood on the table.

'Looks like he's tried to drink himself

to death,' Daley said without any hint of sympathy. 'Reckon we ought to come back another time. We won't get much sense out of your brother for a few hours.'

'I can't leave him like that,' Jack protested. 'Help me get him on to a bed.'

The drunken man did not stir as the two lawmen carried him through to an adjacent room and dropped him unceremoniously on to a bunk.

It was almost an hour later by the time they managed to get Clay into a state where he could speak with some sense and when it came it was nothing that his brother had expected to hear — a craven apology.

'I've been a big fool, Jack and I'm sorry for it,' he slurred. The two men perched on the edge of their seats while Clay Crawford told them his story.

★   ★   ★

Darkness was closing in on the large ranch house when Clay Crawford suddenly realized for the first time that his life was like the house. Empty.

Lucy Dillon had walked out on him; his brother, unexpectedly back from a war in which Clay had never believed, was now the lawman in the town where the name of Crawford was spoken in hushed tones bordering on contempt. Even his partnership with Vic Bannon was held together by nothing more than a thin thread.

He had been drinking alone when he heard the sound of approaching horses. Probably a couple of cowhands back from the range, he reflected, making no attempt to leave the comfort of his armchair. But he was wrong. He had two surprise visitors — and he was not happy to see either of them. Blake Bannon and Zeke Emmett were two of the Lazy-L crowd he had to suffer because of the partnership with Vic Bannon.

They marched into the room as though they owned the place. All smiles and geniality.

And they were drunk.

'Howdy, neighbour. The thought of you sitting here all alone in this big house was too much so we thought we'd come along and cheer you up,' Blake laughed, reaching for the decanter of whiskey on a cabinet shelf. 'Reckon we could maybe have a game of five draw, what d'ya say?'

Clay didn't want company, especially the company of young Bannon and Emmett but he had no choice. They were not going to leave before daylight and by that time all three would be too drunk to care.

Clay looked up at his brother and the man at his side, US Marshal Bob Daley. His voice was little more than a croak when he eventually spoke after a long pause after recalling the events of the previous night.

'After our folks were butchered by those rebels I was desperate. You were gone, Jack — I thought you had been killed — and the ranch was falling apart around me. I was troubled by rustlers, grabbing what beef they could get with nobody to stop them. Cowhands walked out until only three or four were left and they only stayed out of loyalty to Pa.

'Then I heard that the Lassiters had sold out to some money man from Arkansas. It was Vic Bannon. Once he had settled in, Bannon came to see me about having a stake in this place. I asked him if he wanted to buy me out but he said that wasn't in his plans for the time being.'

Clay looked around as if in search of a whiskey bottle but the visitors had put them well out of reach.

'I was desperate so I had to listen to what he had to say. It sounded good. He would pay to rebuild the burned-out house and I could stay on to run the place. He would send in some men to help and when the time came he would buy me out at a price more than I would get from anybody else. Or I could repay him.'

Jack got to his feet and walked

towards the window. He looked out across the pastures where a small herd of cows were enjoying the morning sun.

'What was he wanting from you?' he asked, still hardly able to believe that his brother had suddenly had a change of heart. That a night's drinking was enough to bring him to his senses.

'He said he could use my knowledge to get to know the people of Creek Forks, to see how he would fit in. I guess he was using me as his way to get the local folk on his side.

'At first it all went well. He made big promises and when he needed my help to make them happen I did what I could.'

'Like buying out Alice Bailey's place?' Jack interrupted, his voice heavy with scorn.

Clay didn't answer other than with a nod of the head.

'Most people took a liking to Vic Bannon,' he said. 'He bought out the bank, he took over the Flag Hotel and he opened new stores in town — '

'And closed others,' Jack said, his voice still full of sarcasm but Clay ignored the interruption.

'The trouble is Vic's son — Blake. He's no good, Jack. Him and his friend, Zeke Emmett. They're a bad pair.'

'And you spent the whole of last night drinking with them and playing cards,' Bob Daley put in.

Jack waited for his brother to go on but Clay seemed reluctant to add to what he had already said. Instead, his eyes darted left and right as he searched for the comfort of a whiskey glass.

'I've heard about this Emmett,' Daley prompted him. 'But I'd like to hear more.'

Clay slumped into his chair.

'Like I told you, they came calling last night,' he said eventually. 'They said they were just being neighbourly and that was how it started. We had a few drinks, talked about Vic and me and our plans for the valley and then Blake said something that made Emmett laugh but made me angry. Maybe it was the drink, or the fact that young Bannon is a spoilt kid.'

He paused — he had not lost that haunted look of a man desperate for a drink.

'Go on, Clay,' Jack encouraged his brother.

'He sneered when I tried to explain that his father and I were planning to have the biggest ranch in Missouri. Then he said: 'Don't forget, Crawford, you're only here because of my old man's good will; because he thinks he owes you.'

'I asked him what he meant by that and he just scoffed. 'Maybe one day I'll tell you,' he said, 'but for now, it's best you just do what we say and keep the old man happy.''

'They left soon after that but not before Blake had another sneer. On his way out he turned and said: 'Don't think the Horns are going to be the last people to cross the Bannons, Clay. Remember that the next time we come calling.''

'I came back inside and drank a few more whiskeys and beers until I was, well, on my way to how you found me.'

Jack silently studied his brother. He looked a pitiful wreck, sitting head bowed on the edge of his bed. His mind went back to the days when they were kids together. What had happened to the spirited older brother who had taught him to ride, to rope and to shoot? The boy who had been a natural to succeed his father at the Circle-C when the time came? Now, he was a sorry sight, ruined by liquor and a loss of self respect.

Jack suddenly reached a decision. He could no longer stand by and see his brother suffering like a kicked dog. It was time to act. It was time to tell Ben Lockhart that he was turning in his badge and returning to the Circle-C.

He leaned forward and put his hand on his brother's shoulder. Clay sat silently while Jack outlined his plan which would start by breaking his links with the Bannons and the Lazy-L.

'We can make this work, Clay. The Circle-C can be a Crawford ranch again. Our parents would have wanted that.'

Bob Daley stood aside as the two brothers embraced; a touching moment, he thought. But he had more important things to think about than a brotherly re-union. He wanted to know more about Zeke Emmett.

*　*　*

It was late afternoon when the Crawford brothers, accompanied by US Marshal Bob Daley, arrived at the Lazy-L.

Vic Bannon stepped outside to greet them but he kept any hint of a warm welcome well hidden. Clay Crawford was not a regular visitor and the company he was keeping did not inspire him to think that this was a social call. There was no offer to go inside the house when the visitors dismounted. Bannon tried a formal greeting.

'Evening, Clay, I hope you haven't brought the law along on official business.'

'Howdy, Vic. You've met my brother Jack. This here is Bob Daley, a US marshal up from Carthage. He is looking to talk to one of your hands.'

'Which one?'

'Emmett,' said Daley coldly.

'Zeke?' Bannon tried to look and sound surprised. 'What you want with him, Marshal? He's my foreman. What's he been doin' I don't know about?'

Bob Daley chuckled.

'Well that sort of depends, Mr Bannon. What do you know?'

Vic Bannon was not sure he liked what the lawman was insinuating. US Marshals did not come all the way down from Carthage looking for a man like Zeke Emmett unless they had something to lead them there.

'Well, you're out of luck, Marshal,' he said at length. 'Zeke is out on the range somewhere. I don't expect him back until maybe the day after tomorrow. Are you going to be around that long?'

'Reckon not, now that I know my man isn't going to be around for a couple of days. I'll leave you to talk business.'

Daley turned and walked slowly back to his horse. He had no intentions of waiting two days so that Bannon could warn his foreman that the law was on his tail. At first, he had not been sure that he was chasing the right man but Bannon's reaction had confirmed it. Zeke Emmett was the man he was looking for and, unless he was mistaken, was one of the three men who had killed his brother during the bank robbery in Carthage.

* * *

Vic Bannon offered his two remaining visitors a drink but when they both declined he sensed that this was not about to become a social call.

'What's on your mind, Clay?'

Clay Crawford offered a half smile. 'You've met my brother, Jack.'

Bannon nodded.

'The new lawman in Creek Forks,' he said.

'Not for much longer, Vic,' Clay replied. 'As soon as the mayor can swear in a replacement, Jack's turning in his badge and coming home to help me run the Circle-C.'

Vic Bannon made no effort to greet the news with any degree of goodwill. Instead, he said: 'I guess you've explained our arrangement to your brother, Clay. The agreement we made when I came here to Creek Forks was your idea as well as mine.'

'He has explained,' Jack said coldly. He had taken an early dislike to Bannon. 'We're here to try to change things. I know you helped Clay out when he needed it but you will get your money back. We just need some time.'

Bannon was silent for a moment before turning back to face the brothers.

'I'm really sorry to hear that, boys. We've got an agreement and that says I kept you on to run the Circle-C. There is nothing about you wanting to take it back. I put a lot of cash into that place and we have big plans to turn the valley into the biggest ranch in the county and Creek Forks into a major cattle town. Now you are wanting to go back on all those plans. I don't reckon I can let you do that, Clay.'

'Things have changed, Vic. My brother's home and together we can make the Circle-C what it was. I owe you, Vic, but I'll get you your money back.'

'Things may have changed for you, Clay, but not for me. If you can't stick to our arrangement then you have got to move out.' With that, he turned away leaving the two brothers speechless. Then, he added: 'I'll give you two days to get out — then I'll be moving my men in.'

Zeke Emmett pushed the woman away, gently at first and then, when she did not move, more brutally. 'Get out of here!' he snarled. 'You'll be wanted downstairs.'

'But, you promised . . . ' she started to protest but then, noticing the scowl on his face, thought that now was not the right time to remind him of promises and snatched up her robe and left to head for the casino where she would undoubtedly attract the attention of men who would pay for what she was offering that pig for free.

Like the rest of the ranch-hands at the Lazy-L, Zeke had never been slow to make full use of the room that was always available — paid for by the big boss, Mr Bannon.

It was not that Zeke was not grateful for this little bonus but the time had come to move on. He was sick of playing nursemaid to Blake Bannon, doing his dirty work for nothing more than the thrill of seeing men like Caleb Jones and that old man Horn grovel.

And then, of course, there had been that drunk of a sheriff Luke Franklin. Zeke allowed himself a smug smile of satisfaction at the memory of that night when he stood in the shadows and watched when Franklin walked through his office door to find the place ransacked and Blake pointing a gun at his chest.

Franklin and his dark little secret hidden away in a locked drawer.

The fool spoke too much when he was full of whiskey — which was often — and he got greedy. Drink and greed. They were the reasons to take special care of those papers for him and why Blake had smashed up the room all for nothing, Zeke thought.

But that was in the past. Now it was time to move on. The US marshal in town from Carthage was getting too close. With the phoney reverend out of the way that left only himself and Blake Bannon. It was time to head south and to Texas.

Locking the room door, he dragged

the bed away from the wall, pulled back the rug and took out his knife. Kneeling, he pressed the blade between two floorboards, eased one free, then another until he had enough space to reach under the boards to pull out the first of three bags he had stashed away.

The first two held notes from the Carthage bank robbery and his share, which now amounted to more than twenty thousand dollars; the third bag contained the documents he had taken from Luke Franklin's office — documents that he planned to use as a farewell gift to the sheriff of Creek Forks. And there were others that he knew would give US Marshal Bob Daley more to think about than rounding up a long-gone stranger who robbed a small town bank in southern Missouri.

He stuffed the papers into a large envelope and scribbled the name 'Jack Crawford' along the back. He loaded his saddle-bags, checked that he had not forgotten anything and then left the

Aces High by way of the back staircase.

Down in the alley, Emmett saddled his horse, made sure that the main street was deserted and then rode towards the guest house owned by Alice Bailey. As he expected, the young kid he had often seen before, Tommy Carter, was sweeping the pathway — he seemed to do that throughout his waking hours — and he pulled his mount to a halt.

'Hey, kid! Over here!' he called. Tommy put down his brush and strolled across to him.

'What you want, mister?'

Emmett leaned over in his saddle.

'Does the town sheriff still live here?'

'Sure. You want him for something cos he ain't in right now.'

Emmett smiled. 'I know that, kid, that's why I'm here.'

He pulled the envelope out of his saddle-bag and tossed it down to Tommy.

'Give him this — tell him it's a present from a friend.'

Tommy caught the package, looked up at the man in the saddle.

'Why don't you give it him yourself? He'll be here soon.'

Emmett straightened up in his saddle.

'I ain't got time to sit here talking. I've got a long ride ahead. But remember to tell him that this is a gift from Zeke Emmett and he owes me. See you, kid.'

With that he dug his heels into his horse and the animal responded. Zeke Emmett headed south out of Creek Forks, a rich man on the run, maybe, but his only regret was that he would have liked to have been around to see how the Bannons handled it when Jack Crawford opened his package.

12

'Where the hell is Zeke?'

Vic Bannon spat out the demand but his son merely shrugged.

'I haven't seen him since yesterday. He said he had some business in town and would be back at the ranch by night fall.'

Vic poured himself another drink. He had already emptied one whiskey bottle since the visit from the Crawford brothers and his mood had not improved. He paid Emmett good money to be around the place and keep his hot-headed son out of trouble. Or, if that failed, take the rap for any trouble Blake landed himself in.

'We got problems,' the old man said at last, 'and I need Zeke.'

Blake Bannon slammed his gloves on to the table.

'Zeke! Zeke! All I ever hear is Zeke!

What about me? I'm your son, aren't I? Why is it always Zeke you need when you've got problems?'

Vic was taken aback by the sudden outburst from his son but he did not show it. Instead, he said: 'I have my reasons, Blake, and one of them is that Zeke is a hired gun. He is expendable. You're not.'

But Blake was not satisfied.

'That's no reason, Pa. Where Zeke goes I go. We're, well, we're like brothers. We look after each other.'

Vic Bannon looked at his son. He felt close to despair that the boy would ever understand. When the time came he would have to kill Zeke Emmett to keep his secret and how would he explain that to Blake?

Finally, he said: 'Well, Zeke's not here so you may get your chance before you know it, son. The Crawfords paid us a visit today and I don't reckon we can count on Clay any longer.

'First light tomorrow morning I want you out there rounding up the men.

We're going to pay a return visit to the Circle-C. And it isn't going to be a friendly call.'

* * *

The Crawford brothers sat opposite each other across a wide oak table that dominated the main room of the Circle-C ranch house, between them a whiskey bottle and two untouched glasses. This was not the time for heavy drinking.

They had ridden in silence from the Lazy-L but now it was time to talk, to make plans. Bannon's threat to force Clay out of his home had to be taken seriously. Jack knew that the Circle-C hands were cowmen, not gunfighters, though he was sure the same could not be said for the men of the new owner of the Lassiter ranch.

Jack studied his older brother. Gone was the drunken bravado, the swagger that had welcomed him on his return home only a few days ago. Was he looking at a different Clay Crawford — the one he wanted to remember?

'Tell me about Vic Bannon, Clay. How did he persuade you to let him get a hold on our home?'

Suddenly, Clay opened up but his voice was unsteady.

'Our home? You left our home more than four years ago, Jack, so you can't know what it was like.'

'Then tell me.'

Clay reached for the whiskey bottle but Jack slid it out of his reach.

'Later, Clay. Tell me.'

Clay slumped back in his seat.

'When we heard you had been killed in some skirmish or other — we were never told where — Pa went to pieces. He couldn't work, just moped around all day, drinking. Ma couldn't handle him and she spent her time crying.

'Then we heard all about that massacre up in Lawrence, Kansas. A hundred and fifty men and boys butchered by Quantrill's men. The whole state of Missouri was at war with each other. Unionists and rebs' — he paused before adding — 'men like you, Jack, fighting a goddamn crazy war over what?'

He grabbed the whiskey bottle and this time he was too quick for his brother. Shaking, he poured himself a long drink and finished it in one gulp.

'After Lawrence, Quantrill and his men scattered far and wide, most of them heading for Texas. But not all of them. Even your Confederate Army disowned them as a group out of control.'

He paused again to pour another drink.

'I was in town when it happened. I should have been back at the ranch. I should have been there when they came. Instead I was in the saloon, drinking, gambling. I spent the night in some rat hole with some woman whose name I couldn't remember.

'When I got back the next day they were dead — butchered. The barn had been burned to the ground, the house ransacked and what cattle had not been killed had been driven off.'

'And nobody saw what happened?' Jack queried.

Clay emptied his glass.

'Oh, somebody saw. Luke Franklin for one. And there were others . . . our friendly neighbours. The flames had people running to see what was happening but by then the raiders were heading south.'

'And nobody came forward as a witness?'

'Grey jackets. That's all anybody said they saw. Rebel soldiers.'

Clay pulled himself together. 'For more than a year I tried to rebuild the Circle-C. Almost single-handed. Sure, I got a bit of help from a few cowhands but the neighbours? They kept well clear.'

'What about Vic Bannon? When did he come along?'

Clay poured another drink and this time Jack made no attempt to stop him.

'The war had been over for maybe six

or seven months when I had a visit from Frank Lassiter to tell me he was selling up and moving out West. He said that the man who was buying his place wanted to meet me. I was desperate so I agreed and Vic Bannon suggested we went into partnership. He had big plans, Jack, plans for the whole valley.'

Jack sensed that his brother was having a fight with his own conscience and the feeling was confirmed when Clay suddenly blurted out: 'So I sold out. I told him that the Circle-C wanted to be part of any big plan.'

'And what did he offer in return for your help, brother?'

Clay did not answer at once, then defensively, he shouted: 'Pa and Ma were dead. As far as I knew you were dead. What else could I do? Yeah, I sold out. I borrowed enough cash to rebuild the barn and the house, to restock and to pay the men.'

'And what did Bannon want for his money, Clay? What did you pay him?'

'Vic Bannon got the deeds of the

ranch,' he said without a flicker of emotion. Clay tried to explain. They would be partners; Vic needed him to persuade the others, the farmers and homesteaders, to sell up and move out. When that was done and the plans were in place Clay would have enough money to pay back the loan.

But they had reckoned without Alice Bailey. She rallied the people around Creek Forks and they stood together, even when Clay, using Bannon's money, bought her out and when Vic Bannon took over the bank and refused loans to anybody who needed them.

'And that's when Bannon and his men turned to force,' Jack suggested.

'That's right. And I went along with it. I agreed to bring in that crooked lawyer Tibbs with his fake papers. I didn't say anything when Bannon's kid started roughing up people. I left it to Luke Franklin but he knew the Bannons from way back so he looked the other way.'

It was Jack's turn to reach for the

whiskey bottle but he checked himself. Drinking would not solve anything. From what he had learned, his brother had willingly signed away the Circle-C in return for a loan from Vic Bannon. And Bannon was now calling in that loan. It was clear that the ranch was no longer the Crawford family home and however much Clay tried to blame circumstances and bad luck, the reason for it all was not hard to find.

He had taken the easy route and joined forces with a stranger whose sole purpose was to build himself an empire. He did not think it would help but Jack decided to have that drink after all.

* * *

Tommy Carter was tired. He wished he was in bed instead of sitting there on the steps of Alice Bailey's guest house waiting for the sheriff to arrive home. He had a message to deliver and the man had said it was important. He still had the packet tucked inside his shirt, keeping it safe.

The streets of Creek Forks were deserted at that hour — Tommy had no idea what the time was but he guessed it must have been near to midnight — and there were lights only in a few windows. One of them was down the street in the jailhouse but Tommy knew that it was not the sheriff who was in there. It was the US marshal he had seen around town and he was probably also waiting for Jack Crawford to come back.

Tommy decided. If the sheriff did not come in the next five minutes — he could guess how long five minutes was — he would take the packet down to the marshal and let him pass it on to the sheriff. He yawned. The minutes ticked by and he found himself dozing off, only to be roused out of his slumber by a shake of his shoulder. He looked up into the face Mayor Ben Lockhart who was smiling down at him.

'You should be in bed, young man,

'not out here sleeping on the doorstep.'

'I-I'm waiting for the sheriff,' Tommy stammered. He had always been a bit frightened of important people and they did not come much more important than the town's mayor.

'You can see him tomorrow,' Lockhart said, lifting the boy to his feet.

'But I've got a message for Mr Crawford and the man said it was important.'

'What man?'

'The man who gave me the message. An ugly man,' Tommy added by way of explanation. 'He rode off out of town. Said he couldn't wait but the sheriff would want to know.'

'So, what's the message, Tommy?'

The boy reached inside his shirt and pulled out the brown packet. 'This is it. I don't know what it says.'

Lockhart reached for the envelope but Tommy pulled it away.

'Don't worry, son. I'll pass it on to the sheriff; he's a friend of mine. It will be safe with me.'

Tommy hesitated. The ugly man had

entrusted it to him and he had promised to deliver it.

'Well, if you are sure, Mr Mayor but I really am tired and I don't know when he will be back.'

Reluctantly, he handed over the message but before running off he felt brave enough to say: 'I'll ask the sheriff tomorrow if he got the message.'

Ben Lockhart grinned. 'Trust me, Tommy, he'll get it. But this man, the one who gave you the message. Did he have a name?'

Tommy thought for a moment, then said: 'Funny sort of name . . . Zac . . . no Zeke . . . I don't remember the rest.'

'You're sure? That's what he said?'

'I-I think so.'

Lockhart stood aside and waited for the boy to go inside before stuffing the packet into his pocket and heading for the sheriff's office.

Zeke Emmett. Why would a Lazy-L ranch-hand and friend of the Bannons leave an important message for the sheriff?

Meanwhile he, too, wanted to give Jack Crawford a message. And what he had heard earlier could not wait until the next morning.

★ ★ ★

Ben Lockhart paced the floor of the sheriff's office, looking frequently at his pocket watch and then the wall clock, trying desperately to keep his fraying nerves and his growing fears under control.

If Jack Crawford did not return before dawn it may be too late.

From what he had overheard earlier in the bar of the White Horse saloon — well out of the reach of the prying eyes and ears of the regular clientele at the Aces High Casino — the farmers and homesteaders were preparing to arm themselves and follow the adage that attack is the best form of defence. They were not going to wait for Bannon and his hired guns to run them off their land. Instead they were planning to join together and force Bannon out of the valley. Mayor Lockhart feared that a range war was only hours away.

The other man waiting for the return of Jack Crawford — US Marshal Bob Daley — shrugged at the mayor's fears.

'It's not my fight, Mr Lockhart. I came here in search of three bank robbers who gunned down my brother in Carthage. Your best move would be to telegraph Fort Dawson, get yourself some army help to quell any threat of a range war. The government does not look kindly on its citizens going around shooting each other — not with four years of bloodshed still fresh in the memory.'

Lockhart nodded.

'But that doesn't help us here and now, Marshal, and if the farmers do carry out their threat then Jack's brother is sure to be on their list. They blame him as much as Bannon for what has happened in Creek Forks.

'We saw enough brother against

brother in the war and it is not right,' Daley agreed. 'But, like I said, this is a local dispute and it is not my fight.'

'You can't just walk away,' Lockhart argued. 'You are a US marshal — a peacekeeper.'

They were still talking over the threat when the door opened and the sheriff walked in. At his shoulder was the man they had been discussing — his brother Clay.

★ ★ ★

'But they will be playing straight into Bannon's hands,' Jack said angrily after listening to Ben Lockhart's report of what he had heard in the White Horse. 'He's got the law on his side — and that means me and Bob. If they even set a foot on the Lazy-L land Bannon's men will shoot them on sight and there's not a judge in the land who would convict them. Who the hell has got them so steamed up they want to commit suicide?'

271

The mayor shrugged. 'It sounded like the Dutchman was stirring things and the others were just going along.'

'Then I've got to get out there and stop them,' Jack said, his anger rising. He looked to Bob Daley and his brother for support. Both men nodded. They turned to leave but they had not reached the door before Lockhart called them back.

'Wait, Jack. There's something else you ought to know. It may change your mind.'

He pulled out the brown packet and offered it to the lawman.

'I saw young Tommy Carter sitting on the steps at Ma Bailey's. He had this — said it was a message he had to deliver to you.'

'Who is it from?'

'He wasn't sure . . . but it sounded like Zeke Emmett. Whoever it was left town in a hurry. He told Tommy it was important and I reckon it is.'

'You read it?'

Lockhart nodded. 'I guessed that if it

was as important as the kid was told I might have to come looking for you so, yes, I read it, just to find out. I think you should read it before you go.'

Puzzled, Jack slipped the few sheets of paper out of the packet and read the message written below the official address of the Missouri State Legislature in Jefferson City. It was addressed to Luke Franklin, sheriff of Creek Forks, Missouri and it was dated more than a year earlier.

I wish to report that, following your request for information the following are among the war criminals still at large following arson and murder in Lawrence, Kansas as members of the deserters from the Confederate Army alongside William Quantrill. Although Quantrill himself was killed in 1865 in Kentucky, many of his followers formed their own groups living outside the law. The following are also wanted for raids in Missouri, including the attack you mentioned on the property in your county known as the Circle-C ranch, a raid that included the murder of the owners.

Jack felt his blood running cold as he studied one of the accompanying Wanted bills. Despite the presence of long, unkempt hair and a drooping moustache there was no mistaking the cold, staring eyes. He had added a little weight, the hair was greyer and thinner.

The legend under the image read:

Wanted for Arson and Murder in the States of Missouri, Kansas and Texas. $1,000 Reward.

Alongside the official letter and the poster was a third sheet of paper. A list of names and aliases. And the third name on that list was one they all recognized.

Vic Bannon had been one of the

group who had burned down the Crawford home and murdered Jack's mother and father.

13

Clay moved towards the door but Jack grabbed his arm. He knew instinctively what his brother had in mind.

'Wait, Clay! Leave this to the law.'

The older man shrugged himself free.

'The law!' he sneered. 'Luke Franklin was the law and he knew all about this for more than a year. And what did he do? Don't talk to me about the law, Jack. There's all the proof I need.' He pointed at the sheets of paper that his brother was still holding. 'Bannon and his men killed our folks and now he's back here as though nothing has happened. Well, to hell with your law, Jack. I know what I've got to do . . . with or without your help.'

'No, Clay, hold it.' He remembered the locked drawer and the safe for which he had never been given a key. 'That knowledge got Luke Franklin killed. Vic Bannon could have a dozen or more of those killers out at his ranch. Alone you haven't got a chance.'

But his brother was not listening. He pushed aside the young sheriff and dashed out into the street.

'Stop him!' It was Ben Lockhart who barked out the order but Jack stood frozen to the spot. He was still trying to take in the fact that his father and mother had been butchered by a gang of renegade soldiers led by a man who, only a few hours earlier, his brother had regarded as a close friend.

Marshal Bob Daley pushed past the others and ran outside but he got there only in time to see Clay kicking his horse into a gallop and heading out of town.

★　★　★

Clay felt the rage rising with every stride of his horse as he left the lights of Creek Forks behind them and turned onto the trail to the Circle-C. The

277

darkness swallowed him up and his only guidance was the moonlight, blotted out occasionally by passing clouds. But Clay was not concerned for his safety or that of the horse. He had made this journey many times down the years but this ride was unlike any other.

His own home would be his first stop — a six-gun was no weapon for what he had in mind. He would need much, much more. He believed he would not leave the Lazy-L alive but there was enough of a lust for vengeance in his heart that he cared little about what became of him. His sole purpose in life now was to destroy those who had murdered his family.

Did Jack really believe that now he knew the identity of the man behind that butchery and burning in the fall of '63, Clay would step aside and leave justice in the hands of the law — even law that was led by a Crawford?

Ever since that night, Clay's life had been a series of nightmares. His parents killed, his brother missing in action believed dead, his house burned to cinders by rebel soldiers and his cattle driven off, he turned to drink. And women. Especially Lucy Dillon.

When Vic Bannon arrived to announce that he was buying the Lassiter place and was interested in a share of the Circle-C it was a gift from the gods for Clay.

Bannon was generous in his rebuilding of the ranch house, re-stocking of cattle and even the supply of new hands to replace those who had abandoned the Circle-C after the attack.

But now Clay knew it was all part of a well-planned scheme to get control of the valley he had first visited on a murderous raid four years before.

Another cloud crossed the moon but in the darkness he did not allow the horse to slow its stride and within minutes he was approaching the restored gates of the Circle-C.

There were no signs of life around the bunkhouse or the main building. Although there were four horses in the corral and the embers of a dying fire nearby.

Clay dismounted and headed up the steps into the house. He needed no light to find what he had come to collect — his prize Winchester repeater rifle.

In the shadowy half-light from the moon, Clay spotted the framed family photograph on the desk. He picked it up and studied it for possibly the one hundredth time. It showed his parents, himself and his brother, dressed in their Sunday best clothes. The occasion, he remembered, was Jack's tenth birthday and the family were on their way to the Lassiters' for an afternoon hoedown. Clay himself was close to his fifteenth birthday and had already taken a shine to Lily Lassiter. He stared nostalgically at the photograph for several minutes before returning it to its pride of place on the desk and hurrying from the house.

Outside, the clouds had drifted away and it was a clear, cold night but Clay

Crawford's thoughts were elsewhere. The Lazy-L was little under an hour's ride away. By daybreak he would have carried out his act of vengeance or died in the attempt.

* * *

Vic Bannon lay awake, unable to sleep. He had reached a decision and it was worrying him. Not that he cared too much what happened to Clay Crawford — only fate had spared him back in '63 when Bannon and his men had raided Creek Forks after splitting from Quantrill. It was the relish with which his son Blake had greeted the news that the time had arrived. It was what he had been hankering for ever since he had been made aware of the plan to rid the valley of the farmers and smallholders. And Clayton Crawford.

Bannon reached out for the unfinished whiskey on the bedside table and drained the glass. He knew Blake was a hothead — the bank raid with Zeke

Emmett and that phoney reverend in Carthage was a result of boredom — and relished the war stories, tales of the raids, of Quantrill and his father's heroics, especially at Lawrence, Kansas. But he had never been told of the raid on Creek Forks, Missouri.

But Blake was nothing without Zeke Emmett and that meant another problem for Vic. Where the hell was Zeke?

Bannon's thoughts were interrupted by a loud banging on the bedroom door. He swung his feet over the side of the bed and, as a matter of habit, pulled out the Colt from its holster hanging on the corner post.

'Pa! You'd better come — we got visitors.'

Visitors? In the middle of the night? Puzzled, Vic Bannon pushed the gun into his belt and followed his son on to the landing.

'Who the hell's calling at this hour?'

'It's the sheriff and that US marshal,' Blake told him. 'I was out on the porch when they rode up.'

'Did they say what they wanted?'

'Nope — 'cept that it was important. What can it be, Pa?'

Together they walked down the winding staircase, father and son, shoulder to shoulder, just how Vic Bannon had always wanted it to be. But not like this, with the law closing in.

He knew there could only be one serious reason for two lawmen to be calling in the middle of the night and it also explained why Zeke Emmett was nowhere to be found.

He had betrayed them. Whatever secrets Luke Franklin had locked away in his office, Emmett had taken the night the sheriff was killed. He had wondered who had shot Franklin and now he knew. It must have been Zeke.

While Franklin lived, Bannon had paid for his silence. But now . . . Zeke Emmett was the man who held all the aces. Had he passed them on to the law? Bannon did not wonder for long. It was clear that Zeke had made his getaway and bought himself all the time he needed to make a clear run out of the state — to Mexico.

Jack Crawford could see from the look on the old man's face that he knew why they were there. And that the kid did not.

'Are you going to come along peaceful like, Mr Bannon?'

It was the marshal who spoke. Bannon nodded.

'The boy knows nothing about this, Marshal. He ain't done nothing.'

'That's not true, though, is it?' Jack interrupted. 'He killed that young kid Lester Thomas. Remember? And he can tell us about Luke Franklin.'

Blake looked at his father. There was panic in the eyes.

'Easy, son. It's me they want. Isn't that true, Sheriff?'

Jack felt his jaw muscles tighten. He had to keep a grip on his feelings as he stood face to face with the man who had been responsible for the murder of his parents, burned his house to the ground and here he was trying to do a deal for his own son's life.

'I'm taking you both in. And for two reasons: to see that you get something you don't deserve — a fair trial — and to stop a range war. Somewhere out there more than two dozen farmers and their friends are plotting to run you out of the valley. There will be more bloodshed. You and your son may die, I may die, some of your men and many of my friends will surely die. And for what? A few more acres of land and a thousand head of beef.'

Vic Bannon's smirk turned to a full-blown laugh.

'Ask your brother, Sheriff. Ask Clay what it was for. He was happy enough to go along, to ease his conscience and believe that Frederick Tibbs had the papers to turn those lousy land-grabbing sodbusters out. We — Clay and me — we offered them more than their shacks and their miserable lives were worth.

'Yeah, he was happy enough with the way things were working out until you showed up. Then he went all pious. I'll come with you but I won't be standing alone in that courtroom. I'll have your brother right there beside me. And when they hear about the part he played in the killing of the Horns how do you reckon the folk of Creek Forks will take that?'

'It's you we're here for,' Daley snapped. 'And you know why. And it ain't got anything to do with Clay Crawford and your fight with the farmers.'

*   *   *

Blake Bannon looked scared. Gone was the swaggering bluster, the sneering and snarling that he reserved for the homesteaders.

His father's look of resignation suggested that this was more than just an unwelcome night visit — things he had got used to when Luke Franklin was alive. But this wasn't Franklin turning up for his latest pay-off. This was law that his father's money could not buy.

He looked anxiously at his father.

'What do we do, Pa?'

Before Vic could answer, Daley said: 'I suggest you take your old man's advice, kid and come along with us.'

The marshal moved forward and, with a mixture of fear and panic, Blake reached for his gun. But he was too slow. Daley grabbed his wrist, spun him round and sent him crashing over a desk and into a wall.

He helped the young man to his feet and relieved him of his gun before pushing him roughly towards where his father was standing quietly alongside Jack.

Vic put his arm around the boy's shoulder.

'We go with them, son, but don't worry. We'll have this all cleared up by morning.'

Blake did not look convinced. Cleared up? What was there to clear up? Sure, he'd shot the kid and he'd killed the Horns and that blackmailing sheriff, but that was not why the law was here tonight. There was something else . . . something the old man was not telling him.

'Listen to your father, Blake.' Jack moved forward to grip the younger Bannon by the arm. 'You've got a better chance with us than you would with a lynch mob. And that's the way the folk feel about the Bannons right now.'

And a better chance than your old man gave my father and mother, he thought but said nothing. It was clear that Blake did not know what his father and others had done back in '63.

Reluctantly, Blake allowed himself to be led away but the four had only reached the veranda when the first shot was fired — the rifle bullet splintering the wood of the porch fence.

A second bullet smashed the ranch house window as Vic pushed his son to the boards and dived for cover.

'Who the hell . . . ?' Vic snapped but Jack knew the answer even before the owner of the Lazy-L could finish the question.

It had to be Clay.

Another rifle shot shattered more glass.

Bob Daley spun round: 'Whoever is out there has us as sitting targets with those lamps shining from the house.'

Scrambling inside, the marshal doused the lights, plunging the whole area into total darkness and hurried back outside where Vic Bannon was screaming his anger at Jack.

'Give us a gun, Sheriff. We ain't just gonna sit here to be picked off by some crazy man with no way to fight back.'

Jack ignored him. 'Keep a watch on these two, Bob — I'm going out.'

'Are you crazy? Whoever is out there will gun you down.'

'I know who's there,' Jack said, striding out into the darkness. He had gone no more than fifty paces when the order came from out of the blackness.

'That's far enough, Jack. Not one more step.'

Jack Crawford carried on walking.

'What are you going to do, Clay? Shoot me? Like the others?'

'Stay out of this, brother. And tell that marshal friend to get clear. You know why I'm here. Bannon killed our folks.'

Suddenly, from back at the house, a gunshot caused the brothers to duck instinctively. But neither man was the target. It was clear to Jack that the marshal was in trouble.

He turned and ran towards the house but another gunshot — this time aimed in his direction — forced him to dive for cover behind an abandoned cart. As he crouched, gun in hand and trying to make out the shadowy figures on the veranda, Jack could only guess what was happening.

The Bannons must have jumped Bob Daley, catching him by surprise. But there was no time to think about that as another bullet missed by inches, smashing into a rock behind his left shoulder.

Bullets flew wildly wide of their

target as the two fugitives rode off at top speed into the security of the night. Jack holstered his gun and raced up to the house where he found Bob Daley clutching his shoulder.

'The kid caught me by surprise, Jack,' he gasped. 'He had one of those lady guns in his boot.'

Jack examined the wound. 'You hurt bad?'

'No. Don't worry about me. Grab yourself a horse and get out after them.'

Jack shook his head. 'They'll be long gone by the time I get saddled up.'

He slumped on to a step.

'We'll get you back into town and let the doc patch you up. Tomorrow we'll round up a posse. We'll track them down, Bob. Right now I've got another problem.'

Daley studied him. 'So, it was Clay out there doing the shooting?'

Jack nodded. 'It was Clay and he's mad enough to kill them on sight if he goes after them tonight.'

He was about to suggest that his brother

could well be chasing after the Bannons as they spoke when he suddenly emerged from the darkness, walking slowly, droop-shouldered, towards the house.

'You won't need to go after them, Jack. They'll be back.'

Ignoring the injured marshal, Clay led his brother up the steps into the house.

Re-lighting one of the lamps, Clay strode across the far corner of the room and knelt in front of a low cupboard. Opening the door, he revealed a safe.

'I may have been Vic Bannon's partner but I never trusted him. This is why.'

He pulled open the heavy door and held the lamp in front of the open safe.

'Vic and Blake will never run out and leave all of this,' he said, pulling out a thick wad of notes and waving them in Jack's face. Inside there were rows of the same, plus bags that Jack guessed could only contain gold.

'I reckon there's the best part of eighty thousand dollars here, Jack. The

Bannons will be back for it.'

Jack was not convinced. 'They would guess we'd be waiting for them. They would be walking straight into a noose.'

But Clay waved the protest aside.

'You're forgetting something, brother. They don't know I have found out it was Vic who led the raid of those deserters who torched the Circle-C and killed our parents. As far as they know it was some angry farmer out there doing the shooting. They think I'm still with them.'

He could see that Jack was not convinced but he pushed on: 'Listen, brother, we've got a lot of making up to do and we can't do that until the Bannons are at the end of a rope for killing our parents.'

Jack started to protest but Clay held up his hand. 'Get the marshal back to the doc and round up your posse. I'll wait here. They won't come back tonight. Remember, Jack, I know the Bannons; they won't leave this much money behind. They'll wait their chance and they will come back. Maybe tomorrow. Maybe the next day — but they will come back.'

He watched his brother and then said: 'Please, Jack. Chasing them will be a waste of time. This way we can be sure they won't escape again.'

Eventually, the young sheriff nodded, hugged his brother and moved away. Clay watched as he led two horses out of the corral, saddled up and helped Bob Daley to climb up. He stood on the veranda as the two lawmen disappeared into the night.

When he was convinced they were well out of range he hurried back inside the house, picked up a valise from the table and began stuffing it with wads of notes and the bags of gold nuggets. Then he carried it outside and walked across to where he had left his horse during the shooting. Tying the bag to his saddle and double checking its security, he saddled up and turned his horse away from the direction taken by his brother and the injured marshal.

Clay Crawford knew exactly where to

find the Bannons and what he had to do. And when he had finished he would need all that eighty thousand dollars could buy.

14

The abandoned shack on the edge of the Lazy-L land appeared to be in darkness but as he dismounted on the ridge above the clearing Clay Crawford knew that the place would not be deserted. Vic Bannon and his son would be inside.

Blake and Zeke Emmett had used the shack twice before — both times following bank raids across the Kansas border. Vic had tried to keep quiet his son's involvement in a string of robberies but Emmett never knew when to keep his mouth shut and the day Clay chanced upon the pair, together with that phoney preacher, sharing out their loot, the secret was out.

Clay was angry at first but when the anger faded he replaced it with a feeling that the knowledge of that hideaway would be useful to him one day.

That day had arrived.

Sliding his rifle out of its sheath he checked it was fully loaded before making his way down the hillside towards the shack.

He guessed he would never be able to square things with Jack. Too much had changed and their lives had taken different paths. He had sought justification by telling himself that rarely a day passed without his parents reminding him that his young brother was putting his life at risk in the name of the Confederacy while he stayed home to act as nursemaid.

He had been almost relieved when the news came — false though it turned out to be — that Jack had been killed in some skirmish that passed almost unnoticed among the major battles of the war.

Bitterness replaced any hint of sorrow when his parents, instead of turning to him for comfort, pined for their lost son day after day, ignoring the efforts he was making to keep the ranch working and food on their table as more and more hands deserted for the relative security of a soldier's regular pay.

But they were his family and he loved them. And they did not deserve to die like they did. Even if he could not make it up to Jack there was one thing he could do — and now was the time to do it.

Even as he made his way stealthily towards the shack Clay still had one decision to make. Who would get the first bullet?

Maybe Blake. That way Clay would get the satisfaction of seeing Vic feel what it is like to have someone he loved murdered in front of him.

There were two horses tied to a nearby bush and as he approached he could see a dim light was filtering under the shack door.

Clay snapped the rifle into firing position and kicked open the door.

The Bannons were facing each other across a rickety table. Blake had his back to the door and spun round at the clatter from Clay's forced entrance. Instinctively, he reached for his gun.

'Not a good idea, Blake,' Clay snapped. 'A better one is just to sit and listen.'

Even in the feeble light from the table lamp, Clay could see that Vic was visibly shaken.

'Clay! What — '

The intruder sneered. 'What am I doing here, Vic? Can't you guess? Do you really think I would let you ride out once I had found out what happened? How you got your hands on the Lazy-L. How you used your filthy grey uniform to kill my folks and burn down my home.'

Blake looked at his father.

'What's he sayin', Pa?'

Clay scoffed. 'You didn't even have the guts to tell your own son how you ran out on the rebels — even deserted Quantrill after Lawrence. Then let me tell him, Vic. Let me tell your murdering, bank-robbing son how you killed my family, burned my house to the ground and then came back to try to take over the territory.'

Vic Bannon started to protest but thought better of it. There was little point in trying to convince Clay that things had changed, that it had been war and bad things happen in war. Instead, he remained silent.

'The strange thing is, Vic, I could have killed you earlier tonight but you know who stopped me? Who saved your life? My brother. He was in the way. The sheriff saved your life.'

'It was you out there? Shooting at us. I thought — '

'You thought it was some drunken sodbuster who couldn't hit a barn from ten feet. Wrong again, Vic. No. When I knew that I couldn't get you without my brother getting in the way, I decided to scare you. To force you and Blake to find some way of escaping. You didn't let me down. And coming here, you didn't let me down either. Where else would you go with all that cash and gold just lying about in your safe waiting for you to go back?

'You've made a few wrong calls lately, Vic. Like paying that crook Franklin to keep your secret. He may have been a drunk but he wasn't stupid. He kept those wanted posters and the telegraphs that proved you led the deserters who raided the Circle-C and butchered my folks.'

Clay paused briefly but then said: 'And Zeke Emmett. He was another one of your mistakes. When Blake killed your pet sheriff he was seen. Zeke had already taken all the evidence he needed to hang you, Vic. And now that evidence is in the hands of my brother who wants to take you in to stand trial.

'Isn't that something? A fair trial for the man who killed his folks.'

Suddenly it was Blake Bannon got to his feet and faced Clay.

'You been doing a lot of talking, mister. So what you planning to do — shoot us down here in cold blood?

That makes you no better than us. Just another killer.'

Clay's finger tightened around the rifle trigger. He had not counted on being lectured by a man who had killed a young boy because he was being a pest. But he felt himself wishing that one of them would go for a gun, to give him a reason to kill, a reason to live with himself once this was done. Because, whatever happened next, not all three would be leaving the shack alive.

⋆　⋆　⋆

It was all over in a matter of seconds. Without warning, Blake lunged towards Clay in a desperate but forlorn bid to take control of the situation. Taken by surprise, Clay was sent spinning backwards but the charge cost Blake his young life.

Together the pair crashed against the shack wall and the impact forced Clay to squeeze the rifle trigger.

Blake's screech of pain was short and final as the bullet buried itself deep in his chest. He was dead in an instant, dying in Clay's arms as the pair tumbled in a heap in the corner.

Vic, stunned briefly at the sight of the blood spurting from his son's body, reached for his gun but Clay's action only heaped more pain on the older man. Guessing that Blake was already dead, he pulled the lifeless body on top of him to act as a shield. To his horror, Vic sent a second bullet into Blake's back, ending any belief he still had that his son could survive this horror shootout.

Blinded with rage Vic fired again. This time the bullet missed his son and caught Clay in the side. He got no chance to shoot a third time. Instead, Clay pushed away the dead son and fired a rifle bullet, hitting Vic full in the face.

Breathing heavily, Clay struggled to his feet and walked over to study the almost faceless body of the man who had killed his parents.

Revenge should have tasted sweet but there was no feeling of satisfaction for Clay. He was way past redemption and he knew it. Vic's bullet was buried in his side and he was having trouble stemming the flow of blood. He needed somehow to patch himself up before he could ride any distance.

Outside, his horse, saddled and loaded with money and gold, was waiting to be ridden maybe west to Colorado or Arizona or south to Texas.

Enough money to start afresh. A new life. The Circle-C was his past. There was nothing left for him at Creek Forks.

He looked again at the two bodies, re-checked that there was no life in either of them and turned to leave the shack. Somebody would pass this way soon and find the Bannons but by then he would be miles away from the state of Missouri.

Pulling open the door, he stepped out in to the darkness and found himself staring into the barrel of a six-shooter.

'Planning to go somewhere, Clay?'
Zeke Emmett was grinning.

15

Emmett kept his gun pointed at Clay's chest as the two men faced each other across the table in the dimly lit shack. The two Bannon bodies had been dragged across the floor to the far corner.

'Looks bad, Clay. Reckon you are gonna need a doc to fix up that wound. But leastways you took care of them real good.' Zeke waved towards the bodies in the corner before adding: 'Glad I could be some help.'

He chuckled at the puzzled look on Clay's face.

'Hurting bad, Clay?' He could see the perspiration appearing on the other man's brow. 'Reckon it must be, but I s'pose you'll want to know how I found you.'

Clay didn't answer. Instead, he grimaced, clutched his side in an attempt to stem the bleeding and waited for the man across the table to continue.

'Blake was a young fool who couldn't hold his drink. Three beers and he would let his mouth run off with him so when he told me his pa was paying that sheriff Luke Franklin more than twice what he was worth I knew there had to be a reason. Vic did not spend money he didn't have to so I guessed Franklin must have known something about him that was worth money.

'I found it in his office, some of it locked away in his safe, the rest in a desk drawer — enough to send Vic Bannon to the end of a rope. But then' — he paused — 'you know that, Clay. Your brother told you how Franklin had papers and posters to show that Vic led the rebs who killed your folks. A little present from me.'

He grinned at the look on Clay's face.

'Thought you'd be grateful. I rode out but then I reckoned that maybe I deserved something a bit more than I was getting out of my partnership with Blake and that freak Bart Eaton — Abel Child to you. So I decided to turn back and find out what happened when you Crawfords learned the truth about how your folks died. Must say, you didn't disappoint me, Clay. Following you was easy enough and when you turned up at the Bannons' place I knew that all I had to do was wait.

'So here we are — you with a bullet in your side, those two dead,' he glanced at the bodies in the corner, 'and out there, saddle-bags of money and gold for the taking.'

Clay winced at the growing pain from his gunshot wound. It was worse than he had thought.

'Which leaves you as my only problem,' Emmett went on. 'I could just put another bullet in you and finish what's been started, ride out and not even your brother will ever know what has happened here tonight.

'But I didn't kill those two. Why

would I? They were my friends. Vic didn't burn my house or kill my folks.'

He paused and then chuckled, an ugly sound from a man who held all the aces.

'Then there's that marshal I saw you shoot at on the ranch porch tonight. Sure, I saw that. That guy has been chasing me and Blake ever since a bank raid in Carthage. And from what I know he's not the kind to give up easy. At least not until he's got his man. And that's you, Clay. You're the one he's chasing now. He'll guess you tried to kill him.'

He got up from his chair and walked towards the door. 'So I'll just leave you there and wish you good luck. I reckon if you don't get to see a doctor about that wound pretty soon, it could turn really bad. You may not even live long enough to hang.'

He opened the door and turned. 'Oh, and sorry, Clay, I've a long trip ahead of me so I'll need your horse.'

Without another word, he walked out

of the shack, slamming the door behind him. Clay sat for a moment, heard the sound of horses' hoofs fading into the night before getting to his feet and walking to the door.

He stared out into the darkness. Zeke was right. Unless he got medical help soon the gunshot could turn into something a lot more serious than a bullet wound.

*   *   *

Later the same day Clay Crawford was found, barely alive, by the Lazy-L foreman, who was out on the range looking for strays when he came upon his wounded neighbour. It was almost a day's ride into Creek Forks but Bat Lomax somehow managed to get the injured man back to town and into a doctor's care.

Clay was feverish and his few words made little sense to medical man.

'A shack, Zeke Emmett, the Bannons dead, that was about all I could understand,' the doc told Jack when the young sheriff called in to see how Clay was progressing.

The younger brother was with him when Clay Crawford breathed his last.

★   ★   ★

There were few mourners the day they buried Clay: Jack, US Marshal Bob Daley, Alice Bailey and Mayor Ben Lockhart.

After a brief service and a prayer from the town's new reverend, Jack and Ben Lockhart shared a buggy back to the sheriff's office. On the way, Jack took off his badge and passed it back to the mayor.

'I'll have no more use for this, Ben,' he said quietly. 'I've already hung up my gun for the last time. I don't think I'll be needing a sidearm to run the Circle-C now that the Lazy-L is in the safe hands of the homesteaders.'

A month after starting his new life as a rancher, Jack received a telegram from Marshal Bob Daley informing him that Zeke Emmett had been gunned down during a bank raid in a small Kansas town.

Jack screwed up the paper and threw it into an open fire. He had far more important things to think about than Zeke Emmett's immortal soul. As well as running a busy ranch, he had some serious courting to do.

Jenny Lang would be expecting him.

We do hope that you have enjoyed reading this large print book.

Did you know that all of our titles are available for purchase?

We publish a wide range of high quality large print books including:
Romances, Mysteries, Classics
General Fiction
Non Fiction and Westerns

Special interest titles available in large print are:
The Little Oxford Dictionary
Music Book, Song Book
Hymn Book, Service Book

Also available from us courtesy of Oxford University Press:
Young Readers' Dictionary
(large print edition)
Young Readers' Thesaurus
(large print edition)

For further information or a free brochure, please contact us at:
Ulverscroft Large Print Books Ltd.,
The Green, Bradgate Road, Anstey,
Leicester, LE7 7FU, England.
Tel: (00 44) 0116 236 4325
Fax: (00 44) 0116 234 0205

Other titles in the
Linford Western Library:

NIGHT TRAIN TO LAREDO

Roy Patterson

Visiting Chandler Crossing to take part in its famed poker tournament, Ben Garner finds himself flush with success, and a huge wad of cash. Before he can celebrate, however, he is robbed on the way to his hotel. Desperate and confused, he is suddenly confronted by a mysterious and beautiful woman named Molly Walker. Her offer of a large fee to act has her guard and travel with her on the night train to Laredo seems too good an opportunity to pass up. But is this luck, or misfortune?